WITHDRAWN

The BLACK STALLION

and the Shape-shifter

THE BLACK STALLION SERIES

By Walter Farley

The Black Stallion

The Black Stallion Returns

Son of the Black Stallion

The Island Stallion

The Black Stallion and Satan

The Black Stallion's Blood Bay Colt

The Island Stallion's Fury

The Black Stallion's Filly

The Black Stallion Revolts

The Black Stallion's Sulky Colt

The Island Stallion Races

The Black Stallion's Courage

The Black Stallion Mystery

The Horse-Tamer

The Black Stallion and Flame

Man o' War

The Black Stallion Challenged!

The Black Stallion's Ghost

The Black Stallion and the Girl

The Black Stallion Legend

By Walter Farley and Steven Farley

The Young Black Stallion

By Steven Farley

The Black Stallion's Shadow

The Black Stallion's Steeplechaser

The Black Stallion and the Shape-shifter

The BLACK STALLION
and the Shape-shifter

Steven Farley

Random House New York

Copyright © 2009 by Steven Farley

Published in the United States by Random House Children's Books, a division of Random House, Inc., New York.

Random House and colophon are registered trademarks of Random House, Inc.

Visit us on the Web! www.randomhouse.com/kids

Educators and librarians, for a variety of teaching tools, visit us at www.randomhouse.com/teachers

Library of Congress Cataloging-in-Publication Data
Farley, Steven.
The Black Stallion and the shape-shifter / by Steven Farley. — 1st ed.
p. cm.
Summary: Alec and the Black Stallion go to the Irish coast after the horse suffers a racing injury, and while there, they encounter a shape-shifting kelpie that engages them in a race to save the life of a local girl.
ISBN 978-0-375-84531-4 (trade) — ISBN 978-0-375-96531-9 (lib. bdg.)
1. Horses—Juvenile fiction. [1. Horses—Fiction. 2. Supernatural—Fiction. 3. Ireland—Fiction.] I. Title.
PZ10.3.F215Bc 2008
[Fic]—dc22   2008014895

Printed in the United States of America

10 9 8 7 6 5 4 3 2 1

First Edition

To Rosemary
and
Walter Farley

Contents

kelpie (KEL-pee)
noun, a water spirit of Celtic folklore
reputed to cause drownings
(1740, origin uncertain)

ᴄhᴇ ʙᴇᴀᴄh

ᴄhᴇ ʙʟᴀᴄᴋ ꜱᴄᴀʟʟɪᴏɴ raced along the beach at the water's edge, spray flying from his hooves. Alec Ramsay pressed himself flat against his horse's neck. Riding bareback, he was crouching high and tight and perfectly balanced, guiding the stallion with soft pressure from his hands and legs. Slowly he eased the Black out of his gallop, to a trot, and then a walk.

Tossing his head, Alec sat up and flicked his red hair out of his eyes. Gray predawn light shone over the sand dunes on one side of him and the Atlantic Ocean on the other. Out to sea a distant line of fog blurred the horizon where the ocean met the sky.

This was nice, Alec thought. He took in another deep breath of sea air and blinked his tired eyes. He'd been up late last night and barely slept an hour before he and the Black left New York's Belmont Park at four o'clock this morning. After an hour's drive, he arrived at his friend Pete Murray's riding academy, located next to this wildlife refuge on the coast of Long Island. The reason for coming here was to pick up a yearling colt Pete wanted moved up to Hopeful Farm. Alec was vanning the Black back to the farm today, so he'd offered to bring the chestnut-colored colt along with them. But when Pete realized he had misplaced some of the yearling's medical records, he suggested Alec take the Black for a ride on the beach. It would give them something to do while he searched through his files for the missing papers.

Alec looked out to sea, letting his sleepy gaze drift away into the distance. The fog on the horizon was moving closer now. The wind was still. Just offshore a fishing boat motored west toward New York Harbor, trailed by a flock of seagulls.

The weather was cool for early summer, cool enough to send a chill up Alec's back. His shirt was damp with sweat. Seawater dripped from his bare feet and calves. His blue jeans were rolled up to his calves, his shoes back at Pete's stable with the Black's saddle and bridle. Alec slid his hands gently over his horse's neck, warming his chilled fingers in the pocket of warmth under the stallion's mane.

How long had it been since he'd gone for a ride with the Black on the beach like this? Alec asked himself. More than a year at least. Yet somehow it seemed like only yesterday, comfortable and familiar. Alec wondered about that and decided the reason must be because riding on the beach always brought back memories of his first days with the Black, when they were shipwrecked together on a deserted island off the coast of Spain. How could he ever forget that time, his first wary encounters with the Black and their struggle for survival there?

Much had changed since those magical days on the island and his first wild rides on the Black. He had changed. The Black had changed. They were both older now. The Black was a mature stallion, well into his teens, a legend at the racetrack and a proven sire of stakes-winning colts and fillies. Alec was a breeder of horses and a professional jockey with hundreds of rides under his belt. Yet the bond between them remained. It was something unique and difficult to describe, a sense of "oneness" that Alec felt with no other horse. Long ago he'd given up trying to explain it to people, especially those caught up in the hard-boiled, twenty-four-hour, seven-day-a-week world of professional horse racing.

Putting his attention back on his horse, Alec gave the Black a pat on the neck and urged the stallion forward. Ahead of them was a bend in the shoreline. The Black tossed his head, eager to run another mile or so.

"Easy, fella," Alec said, holding the Black to a walk. "We're going to have to turn back pretty soon. Let's just see what's around this bend."

The stallion skipped into motion. Alec gave the Black his head and moved with him, burying his face in the streaming mane. The world sped by in a blur, everything fluid around them, everything in motion. Alec bent himself against his horse and the Black carried him faster and faster, carrying him far away, carrying him all the way back to those first days on the island once again. . . .

When Alec pulled the stallion up finally and turned to look out to sea, the sky seemed darker suddenly, despite the early-dawn light. At first he thought perhaps a storm was blowing in from somewhere. Then he realized the fog he'd seen offshore earlier was much closer now, already sweeping over the rocky point and swallowing up the beach around him. The birds, the fishing boat and everything else out to sea were gone. Ocean and sky blended together into one great field of smoky gray. In seconds the low-hanging mist was so thick that Alec could hear but not see the waves as they washed up on the sand only a few yards away.

"We should head back before we get totally lost in this soup," Alec said, angry with himself for not paying more attention to the changing weather. The Black gave a snort as Alec turned him around and started back toward the point.

As they rode along, Alec noticed that the blanket of fog brought with it a strange quiet. It softened the rumbling surf and the squeaky-wheel crying of the seagulls hovering overhead. Even the blowing of the Black's breath, the swish of his tail, sounded far away now. The misty cushion of fog surrounding them was making Alec feel sleepier than ever.

The Black seemed fascinated by the fog as he moved cautiously along, his ears pricked, his head held high. Alec had sense enough to know that the smart thing to do now was to take it easy and trust the Black to lead the way back. "Okay, big guy," Alec said. "It's up to you now. You get us back to Pete's and I'll do my best not to fall asleep along the way."

They walked another minute through the fog when suddenly Alec could feel the Black tensing up. Instinctively he snapped to attention just as the stallion bounced to a stop. Alec took up a double helping of mane in his fists. The Black threw his head, then rocked back on his hind legs.

"Easy, boy," Alec said, leaning forward to regain his balance. "There is nothing there. Easy now. Probably just some birds."

Alec waited a few moments, then gave the Black a nudge with his heels. The stallion ignored him and remained still, staring intently into the fog. The signals Alec was receiving from the Black now were impossible to mistake. The stiff tension could mean only one thing. Danger.

Alec listened. Maybe someone was there. But who could it be at this early hour? A fisherman? A park ranger perhaps? The disquieting thought crossed Alec's mind that horseback riding might not be totally legal here. Many places on Long Island didn't allow dogs on the beach, much less horses. Surely Pete would have warned him if horseback riding was unlawful on this stretch of beach. Then again, Alec thought, maybe not. Pete could be a real joker sometimes.

The Black pawed the sand and whistled. Alec steadied his horse and listened again. There was something there. Now he could hear it too, a muffled drumming sound, like hoofbeats. Could it be another horse? Alec wondered. Out here?

The idea suddenly occurred to him that Pete might have saddled a horse and come looking for him. "Hey, Pete," he called. "Is that you?"

No one answered.

Alec strained his eyes in the fog and called out one more time. "Pete? Hello? Is anyone out there?"

Again there was no reply, only the pattering sound, coming closer and closer. They were hoofbeats, Alec felt certain now. But where were they coming from? At first the drumming seemed to be coming from the side, then from behind, then in front, then from the direction of the sea. Even the Black seemed confused, tilting his ears one way, then another, as if unable to pinpoint the source of the sound in the pale curtains of sea mist.

A draft of wind brought the odor of seaweed, a smell so sour it caught in Alec's throat and made him gag. Wisps of fog swirled around him. It sizzled and cracked in his ears like the sound of burning grass. From somewhere nearby came a faint sound of tinkling bells, like wind chimes in a breeze.

All at once, the sounds stopped and all he could hear was the lapping of the waves on the shore. Then, from the corner of his eye, Alec saw a shape materialize in the fog beside him. The Black spun around. Startled by the sudden apparition, the stallion screamed and shifted his weight back onto his hindquarters, his body tight as a coiled spring.

It was a girl riding a horse, a magnificent black stallion, one nearly as big as the Black himself, his coat splashed with water and glistening like a raven's wing. The stallion turned to face Alec, slowly, deliberately, its large eyes red-rimmed, wide and staring. The girl rode hunched painfully over the horse's neck, her arms thrust deep into the raven-colored mane. She lifted her head and her long, dark hair fell back from the pale oval of her face. Their eyes met for only a brief moment, but in that instant Alec could plainly see the terror there. Her mouth was open and she seemed to be pleading to him, trying to call out but unable to find her voice.

"Hey," Alec called. "Are you all right?" The girl still did not answer and suddenly the Black threw his head and screamed again. Alec struggled to keep the Black under control as the girl and her horse swept down the beach to vanish among the misty veils of fog. Before Alec knew what was happening his stallion plunged after them. Alec called to the girl again, but the only reply was the sound of splashing in the shallows.

The Black followed the splashing sounds through the shifting layers of mist. Up ahead, Alec could just make out the forms of the girl and her horse moving out into the deeper water. He watched in disbelief as they sank lower, to their shoulders, and then their heads. An instant later the water closed over them and they were gone, leaving only ripples on the surface to testify that they were ever there at all.

Alec stared into the fog, startled and shaken. The Black back-stepped through the water and screamed again. "Easy, boy," Alec said when he found his voice. "It's okay. It's okay."

But it was not okay, Alec knew. He blinked his

eyes. That girl. What happened to her? Blinded by the sea mist, he listened intently for some clue to tell him that what he'd just seen was real. But all he could hear was the crackling of the waves washing over the sand.

From off the land, a sudden breeze rose up. As quickly as it had descended, the fog began to blow out to sea, taking most of the smell of seaweed with it. Soon Alec could see the waves once more. Offshore were birds, the fishing boat, and the fog retreating toward the horizon. But of the girl and the mysterious black horse, he could see not a trace.

2

THE CALL OF THE KELPIE

IMMEDIATELY ALEC BEGAN questioning what he'd seen, or thought he'd seen. Could it really have been a horse, he wondered, a giant of a horse, a stallion so big and perfectly molded that he struck Alec as nothing less than some ghostly reflection of the Black himself? And what of the dark-haired girl? Alec felt certain he'd seen her face before. But where? Try as he might, Alec couldn't place her.

Again Alec scanned the water beyond the shore break for a sign of anything out of the ordinary. Aside from the retreating line of fog, all was tranquil, sea and sky, exactly the same as before.

Back on the beach, Alec slipped down from his horse's back and began to search for traces of hoof-prints in the sand. There were the Black's prints, as recognizable to Alec as his own handwriting. But nowhere could he find a sign of another horse. Alec led the Black over to the water's edge. Perhaps the hoof marks had been washed away by the waves.

Alec walked farther up the beach, searching for tracks in the sand at his feet. Here were the Black's hoofprints again, but nothing else. He shook his head and looked out to the horizon. What happened to that horse? He'd seen him, heard him, even felt the slipstream of wind as he passed by them. And hadn't the Black seen him too? Alec couldn't have mistaken the stallion's reaction. Something had been there. It couldn't have all been just some kind of illusion, some chance convergence of light, wind and wisps of fog. Or could it?

As if sensing Alec's confusion, the Black pawed the sand and stared out to sea. Alec followed his gaze, waiting and watching. The Black lowered his head to press his muzzle gently against Alec's shoulder and then raised his head to look seaward again. Alec took a deep breath to settle his nerves. The air was still tinged with the pungent fragrance of seaweed, the same smell that had seemed so overwhelming only minutes before. Reaching up, Alec knotted his fingers in the stallion's mane. With one quick step he swung up onto the Black's back and then started the stallion toward the point again.

Back at the riding academy, Alec put the Black in a small paddock and then, over a quick cup of coffee, told Pete about what happened on the beach. After Alec finished his story, the squat, square-built ex-jockey just laughed. "Only you could run into a kelpie on Long Island, Alec," he said.

"Kelpie?" Alec asked. "What's a kelpie?"

Pete shook his head in mock disappointment. "Tsk, tsk. All the places you've been, I'm surprised you don't know your own culture. With that red hair of yours, you must have some Irish in you."

Alec shrugged. "I'm part Irish, but my dad doesn't make a big deal of it. What does that have to do with the horse I saw on the beach?"

Pete leaned back in his chair and smiled. "Haven't you ever heard of a sea horse?"

"Sure."

"Not the little question mark–shaped fish you might see in an aquarium. I'm talking about a regular-size horse that can live underwater."

"Of course not," Alec said.

"Well, shame on you, then. When I lived in Ireland, the old-timers used to tell us lots of stories about the Fin Folk, the seal-like selkie people and particularly the kelpies. They're sort of a horse version of a mermaid, or more likely a merman, and usually not a very nice one."

"Merman horses?"

"Sort of, except they're like werewolves too

because at times they can take human form. As horses they tend to run off with children, stranded travelers or anyone else unfortunate enough to climb onto their backs."

"Werewolves? Mermaids?" Alec held up his hands. "Now wait a minute, Pete."

Pete ignored Alec's protest and drew a deep breath. "The thing about your garden-variety kelpie," Pete said earnestly, "is that a person can't get off once he gets on, not until the kelpie dumps him in the water, where the victim usually drowns. Some kelpies eat their unlucky riders, or so the story goes. Others take them down to an underwater kingdom as captives, where they are forced to serve the kelpie until the end of their days. Ask your dad about it. Or better yet, ask Henry Dailey. He has some Irish in him too, if I remember correctly. Maybe he can tell you."

Pete leaned back in his chair and smiled. "But watch yourself, Alec. We don't want you to wind up on the kelpie's dinner menu."

"Okay, Pete," Alec said. "Very funny. But what I saw was no fantasy horse. It was real."

Pete shook his head and barely suppressed a laugh. "Whatever you say, Alec."

"But I saw him," Alec said. "I heard the splashing and . . ."

Pete gave Alec a sly wink. "Ye have horses on the

brain, me boy," he said, putting on his best Irish brogue.

Alec shook his head. It all did seem unbelievable now, Alec thought, and sort of embarrassing too. He began to wish he'd just kept his mouth shut. How could anyone blame Pete for not believing such a story? Alec probably would have thought the same thing if someone told him about seeing a mysterious horse appear out of nowhere and then vanish into the sea.

"Oh, I don't know," Alec said. "You're probably right. It was probably just the fog. It wouldn't be the first time I was so tired I fell asleep on top of a horse."

"You better stay here and take a nap before you head upstate," Pete said.

"I'll be all right," Alec said. "But I will take a thermos of that good coffee of yours along for the ride."

Pete grinned. "I'll make you a fresh batch, extra strong."

"Thanks," Alec said. Pete gave a nod and then stood up from the table. He walked over to the coffee-maker and set to work.

As he waited for Pete to brew up the coffee, Alec picked up a copy of the *Daily News* from the kitchen table. He turned to the sports section and scanned the race results. As he thumbed through the local news, a photograph on one of the back pages caught his eye.

Under the headline "Long Island Teen Still Missing" was another picture of the girl who had vanished at the shore the previous week. Her father was a prominent local citizen and the story about her disappearance had been all over the local section of the paper for the past three days.

But what really caught Alec's attention was something else entirely. Suddenly he knew why he'd thought he recognized the girl on the horse on the beach. Could it really be her? True, he hadn't gotten a very good look at the girl, but it could be the same person: about the same age, the same hair, and a similar profile. But he couldn't really be sure. He thought about telling Pete but then decided against it. He'd made enough of a fool of himself for one morning.

A few minutes later the Black was loaded into the van beside Pete's colt and it was time to go. Waving goodbye to Pete, Alec turned the van out onto the road and started home. He put all thoughts of what had happened on the beach out of his mind and paid strict attention to the traffic around him.

Driving carefully on roads he knew well, Alec soon found that his main concern was simply staying awake. Finally he was pulling off the state road only a few miles from home. A minute later he turned up the long driveway to the farm. Ahead were the horses grazing in wide green pastures, the paddocks, the house and the peaked barns. Each barn was topped with a weather vane wrought in the shape of a galloping black horse.

Alec pulled the van to a stop by the training barn. Both horses were unloaded quietly. Alec tended to Pete's colt first, turning the yearling out in a pasture behind the barn. Then he led the Black along an adjacent walking path, more fencing and a patch of meadow. Soon they came to another pasture where an old gray gelding grazed sleepily under an elm tree. It was Napoleon, the Black's faithful friend and stablemate. The pony raised his head and whinnied a greeting the Black recognized at once. The stallion glanced at Alec, then threw back his head to answer Napoleon's greeting with a high-pitched cry of his own.

Alec opened the gate and unclipped the stallion's halter. The Black burst into motion and cantered off to visit with his old friend. A contented feeling warmed Alec's insides as he watched the Black relax in his familiar stomping grounds. It was always nice to come home again, he thought, even if they had been away at Belmont only a few days.

Following the path to the stallion barn, Alec walked up the aisle toward Satan's stall at the far end of the barn. "Hello, big boy," Alec called as he looked over the half doors. "What's Henry got you penned up in here for?" The burly colt turned his head from the

hay net, where he stood munching a mouthful of timothy hay.

Satan was the pride of Hopeful Farm these days,
a stakes-winning champion with a track record that
ranked even better than that of his sire, the Black.
Though their come-from-behind running styles were
much the same, Alec thought, up close the differences
between Satan and the Black were pronounced. Satan
was heavier than the Black, his neck shorter and more
bulging with muscle. His head was heavier too. And
yet the great, thick body had the same smooth sym-
metry of form, the same proud neck that curved all the
way to delicate ears.

Satan stopped eating as Alec stepped inside the stall.
Alec reached out to give him a scratch on the neck.
Satan sniffed at the sleeve of Alec's shirt, then bobbed
his head and snorted fiercely, feigning wariness, as if
provoked by the scent of the other horses on Alec.
"That's a fine hello," Alec chided playfully. He laughed
and stepped back to let the young stallion have his way
and assert himself.

Alec watched Satan's display of attitude and
shook his head. He was glad he could laugh about it
now. There had been times when the conflict between
Satan and the Black had been deadly serious. Even
now, keeping a truce in effect between the two horses
wasn't easy. A minute later Alec caught up with Henry

Dailey at the training track. Hopeful Farm's head trainer, a tough, leathery-looking old-timer in a well-worn fedora, was leaning over the rail in his usual spot. His eyes were following a pair of horses and their exercise riders coming around the far turn.

Henry grunted, then turned to face Alec. "So what's up, kid?" Henry asked. "How was the ride up from Belmont? How's Pete?"

"Same as ever," Alec said. "I put that colt of his in the back pasture."

Henry nodded. "Is he settling in okay?"

"He seems agreeable enough," Alec said. "I guess we'll see if he's all the horse Pete thinks he is."

"And the Black?"

"He's doing fine. Belmont was great. You know how it is. They always treat him like royalty down there. And the benefit race was a big success. But something odd did happen when we were at Pete's place," Alec said. "I'm telling you, Henry. It was really weird."

Henry arched an eyebrow under the brim of his fedora. "Yeah?"

"Yeah."

"Surprise me."

"Don't think I'm crazy, but have you ever heard of some Irish superstition about horses called kelpies?"

Henry shrugged and returned his gaze to the pair of runners bobbing along the backstretch. "There's a breed of sheepdog called a kelpie, I think. My friend Harry has one."

"No," Alec said. "This is something else. According to Pete it's supposed to be a sort of mermaid horse, lives underwater, like a Loch Ness monster sort of thing."

"Irish, you say?"

"Ireland, Scotland and thereabouts."

"Sounds like Pete's been telling sea stories again," Henry said.

Alec shook his head. "It's not Pete telling this one, Henry. It's me." Alec took a deep breath. "Listen to this. We had some time when we got to Pete's, so I took the Black for a ride on the beach. It was a beautiful sunny morning until the fog came in. Then I saw this horse."

"So?"

"I tell you, Henry, I could have sworn I was looking at a reflection of the Black. He was that much of a horse, the same Arabian head, the same confirmation, the same action when he moved. It was scary. I only saw him for a second or two before he vanished back into the soup. Then I heard this splashing, like a horse running off into the water. When the fog lifted I couldn't find a trace of him, not a hoofprint, nothing. But I swear I saw him, Henry. And there was this girl on his back and she looked just like . . ."

Henry held up his hand and laughed, a reaction that Alec should have expected but somehow didn't. "Oh come on," Henry said. "A horse that looked like the Black? On some beach on Long Island? You better get your eyes checked."

"I saw him, Henry," Alec said.

Henry pondered Alec's story, then shrugged. "I can believe you saw a horse on the beach," he said, "but not one like the Black. Probably some kid from the riding academy out for a morning ride, just like you."

"Not according to Pete," Alec said. "At least he's never heard of a horse boarding in the area like the one I described."

"So maybe you were confused by the fog," Henry said. "What about the Black? How'd he act when you saw it?"

"Like there was definitely something there," Alec said. "He wanted to take off into the water after it."

"What did Pete say?"

"Pete thinks I'm seeing things, like you. Either that, or I ran into one of these Irish kelpies of his."

Henry pushed his hat forward and scratched the back of his head. "Well, that is a bit of a coincidence, the Irish part anyway." He reached into his jacket and pulled out an envelope from his inside pocket. He handed the envelope to Alec. "Take a look at this. It came in the mail this morning."

Alec took the long white envelope. The first things that caught his attention were the unusual stamps and the Dublin postmark.

Dublin? Alec thought. That was Ireland! And the return address was the Irish Jockey's Club. He opened the envelope and quickly unfolded the letter inside. It was an invitation for the Black to come to Ireland, all expenses paid, for a race at a new track that was opening outside Dublin.

"Well, how about that?" Alec said. "You know, I've always wondered what it is like in Ireland. It certainly looks like a nice place in movies and magazines." In his mind he conjured up images of ruined castle towers, of boundless fields of green grass, high cliffs and wide beaches, the Emerald Isle.

Henry chuckled and then began singing wistfully, his voice soft and husky, " 'Oh, when Irish eyes are smiling . . .' Hey, now there's an idea. Maybe we could pick up one of those kelpies of yours. Win some money for a change."

Alec laughed. "A free trip to Ireland, hmm? Sounds like it could be a plan."

"Think so?" Henry asked.

"Hey, I'm just talking," Alec said. "Might be fun.

Someplace to go. Someplace new." Alec glanced at Henry, but the trainer had already turned his attention back to the runners on the track.

It was sort of a crazy idea, going all the way to Ireland just for one race, Alec thought. But he'd always wanted to go to Ireland, not so much because his dad's family hailed from there as it sounded like a cool place. And both he and the Black could use a break. The farm was in pretty good shape financially, the horses healthy, the barn help experienced and trustworthy. Hopeful Farm should be able to survive for a few days without him. Maybe a trip to Ireland wasn't such a crazy idea after all. If only he could get Henry to see it that way.

Up the track, the two exercise riders turned their horses around and started back to where Alec and Henry were standing. "You know," Henry said, turning to Alec slowly, "now that you mention it, a quick trip abroad might not be such a bad idea at that."

Henry's words caught Alec by surprise. "Really?" Alec said. "You're serious?"

"Don't sound so shocked, kid," Henry said.

"I'm not shocked," Alec said, "but you've never been too keen on the idea of going overseas before."

Henry shrugged. "No change of heart, really. It's just that I got a letter recently from my cousin Tom. I told you about him, didn't I? He lives over there."

"Hey, that's right," Alec said. "I'd forgotten that you have family in Ireland."

"Tom is a small-time racetracker, got a little farm out on the west coast," Henry said. "I haven't seen him in, oh, must be close to fifteen years now."

"Have you ever been to Ireland, Henry?" Alec asked.

"No, never made it over there," the old trainer said. "Tom was living in the States when I saw him last. Then he moved back home. He sent me this letter a couple weeks ago, telling me all about this colt he's been training at his farm. He's really hot on him. Might be worth checking into."

"Think so? Really?"

"Sure. If you think the Black is up for it."

Alec nodded. "I'd say we're all due for a change of scene. Who knows when we'll get another chance."

"What is it, five hours' difference between here and there?"

Alec looked at his watch. "Something like that."

"Tom might still be awake," Henry said. "We'll finish here and then go make a phone call."

beyond here be dragons

TWO WEEKS LATER, the Black, Henry and Alec found themselves in a specially designed horse-transport jet taking off from New York's LaGuardia Airport, bound for Dublin, Ireland. Alec was glad that the Fairfield Racetrack officials had arranged a morning flight for the Black, knowing a daylight passage across the Atlantic would make the trip easier.

The Black was hardly the greatest traveler in the world, but so far he was managing the flight well enough. Inside the aircraft, everything was designed for a horse's maximum comfort and safety. Each of the four horses making the trip had his own roomy stall with a soft rubber-matted floor covered with a thick carpet of wooden shavings. The Black's stall was nearest the front of the plane and even a bit larger than the rest.

Alec stood beside his horse, pouring a never-ending stream of kind encouragements into the stallion's ear, reminding him that it would all be over soon, imagining where they were going and all the fun they would have with those extra few days they'd squeezed into their schedule.

After an hour or so Alec walked back to the seating area to see how Henry was handling the trip. The old trainer could be as temperamental about traveling as the Black. Thankfully it looked like Henry had dropped off to sleep in his seat. Alec didn't see any reason to wake him and turned his attention to the scenery out the window of the flying stable. Down below he could see the wide expanses of the Atlantic stretch out for miles.

It sure looked beautiful out there, Alec thought, though sort of lonely too, lonely and mysterious. Hadn't he heard somewhere that scientists said we know more about the surface of the moon than about the bottom of the ocean? No wonder superstitious folks used to people the unknowable depths of the sea with monsters. "Beyond here be dragons," he thought. Wasn't that what was written on the old maps warning folks away from the uncharted parts of the world?

Seven hours after they'd waved goodbye to the New York skyline, the pilot announced that they were nearing the coast of Ireland. The sun was already low-ering to the horizon even though they had left New York at dawn.

Alec peered out of one of the windows but couldn't see anything at first due to the low-lying cloud cover. Then they burst through the clouds and Alec beheld his first glimpse of the Emerald Isle. It was green all right, as green as the felt on a pool table. He saw rivers, lakes, and then everything on the earth below seemed to vanish as they passed into the clouds again. They started their descent, and by the time any-thing was visible on the ground again they were over the suburbs of Dublin.

At last they were on the ground and the aircraft came to a stop. Henry was fussing around outside the Black's stall. Alec stood beside his horse, his attention focused on the stallion and keeping him relaxed and still. It wasn't easy. The Black was wide-awake now and anxious to get out of his stall, rocking on his hooves and pulling against the cross ties holding him.

After deplaning in a special hangar, Alec and Henry passed their customs and immigration inspec-tions. They brought the Black through the gate and were met by a big, smiling man with a shock of red hair. "Tom?" Henry asked. "Is that you?"

"And who else would you be thinking I might be, cousin?" said the smiling man in a hearty, booming voice. He surprised Henry with a bear hug and then turned to Alec and the Black. The stallion held his head up, his clear, wide-set eyes brimming with curiosity.

"Greetings to you, young Ramsay," Tom said, "And welcome to the Holy Land of Ireland." They shook hands. Tom's fingers were work-hardened with smooth calluses. The big man turned to the Black, stepping close, but not too close, to the towering stallion.

"And a fine, beautiful horse you are too, Mr. Black," he said. The stallion was looking around him, arching his glossy black neck. His ears pricked warily and he flared his nostrils, sensing for clues to all that was new here. Alec kept his hand on the Black's halter, paying strict attention to his horse as a group of onlookers pressed closer.

All at once the Black half reared and the gathering crowd backed off. Alec watched the crowd scatter and smiled. Let them stay back, he thought. A person didn't have to look long at a horse like the Black to know that he was a horse to be respected, if not feared. To Alec, the fact that the stallion could be so dangerous made him love the Black all the more. It kept him alert, kept him focused on his horse, and that was always good, especially in public.

Soon Tom was plying Henry with questions about

the trip, life back in the States and Hopeful Farm. He asked Alec about the Black and talked about the bright prospects of the upcoming event at Fairfield. It didn't take long for Alec to realize that Tom was as charming and talkative as Henry could be tight-lipped and critical.

The Black was checked by a vet, given a clean bill of health and then transferred to Tom's van for the trip to the racetrack. Alec rode in the back of the van with his horse while Henry rode up front with Tom.

"America," Tom mused aloud as he drove along. " 'Tis a lovely place." He tilted his head back and called to Alec through the partition window. "Ah, Alec, me boy, you was just a wee lad when I last laid eyes on her fair shores."

"It's changed some over the years," Alec called back.

"And how," Henry said. "You'd hardly recognize the old neighborhood back in Flushing anymore. Why, I tell you, Tom . . ."

Alec tuned out as Henry began his all-too-familiar rant, to Alec at least, about the degenerating state of the modern world, the pollution, the noise and the general decline in civility. Henry's commentary was soon lost in the din of the passing cars. The Black raised his head to the window, and Alec turned that way too. His hand moved to the stallion's neck, then to his ear. The Black dropped his head to enjoy the caress, nudging Alec in the chest.

The highways outside Dublin seemed the same as any other city, crowded with cars and trucks. Big cities were all the same somehow, Alec thought as he stared out the window, everyone in a hurry, with places to go and things to do. Here everyone was driving on the left-hand side of the road, and Alec was glad he wasn't the one behind the steering wheel.

Before long they were passing suburban housing developments, older houses and cottages, even a ruined castle covered with dark-leaved ivy. Here and there low walls of gray stone crisscrossed green hills and valleys. The late-afternoon sun bursting through the clouds made everything all the more verdant and spectacular in the rare sunlight.

A slanting, lime green roof capped by high white spires came into view as they neared Fairfield Racetrack. The van slowed and stopped at the gate. Tom showed his pass to the guard and drove the van to where rows of barns lined the back side of the track. They followed the driveway to a barn where they could unload the Black. Then Alec turned the stallion loose in a large paddock so he could shake out the kinks in his legs. After that they took the Black to a well-appointed stall stocked with fresh hay, water and a ration of sweet oats.

Once the Black seemed more interested in his food than pacing the floor of his stall, Tom took Henry to their rooms at a trackside motel. Alec stayed behind to shower in the jockeys' locker room and spend the night on a stable cot outside the Black's stall. Certainly the barn was safe enough, but it always made Alec feel better to know that his horse was secure and settled in whenever they were in a new place.

That night, as he lay on his cot trying to sleep, he heard the sound of soft music coming from up the barn aisle. It was a radio tuned to a music station, and Alec recognized the song that was playing, an American R & B classic that had been a favorite of Pam's.

Alec tossed in his blanket and thought of his Pam, the girl he'd loved and lost. A tremor of sadness pulsed through his heart. How long had it been? How many months and days? It seemed like only yesterday that he'd learned she was gone forever, the victim of a tragic car accident in the Austrian Alps. Alec listened to the music and tried to remember the good times they'd had together. What else could he do?

The next morning, after a quick cup of coffee and a buttered roll in the track employees' cafeteria, Alec brought the Black out of his stall, gave him a light grooming and tacked him up. Soon they were walking along the path that led between the barns to the turf oval. The Black was feeling good, Alec could tell, all up on his toes and full of himself. Alec was feeling good too and adjusting well to the five-hour time difference between New York and Ireland. It helped that most everyone he met seemed friendly, quick with a smile, a nod of the head or a pat on the back.

As they reached the track, Alec saw the looming grandstand, empty now save for a handful of spectators scattered about watching the morning workouts from the ground-level seats and at rail-side. The path led to a gap in the fence, and a moment later they were stepping out onto the track. The Black jogged ahead, ears pricked, all tight and right and ready to go.

Like most tracks in Europe, the new Fairfield Racetrack was primarily a turf course. The footing was good, soft but springy in a way that was different from the grass on the inner turf course at Belmont. Alec loosened his hold on the reins and soon had his hands full keeping the Black to a slow gallop.

Fairfield was a fairly regular-shaped oval track, with a wide, flat surface, much like a standard American track. On his second circuit of the grass oval Alec recognized Henry and Tom among the railbirds watching the Black and the other horses out for their morning jogs. Tom waved as Alec galloped the Black past. Henry nodded, but even from a distance Alec could see the old trainer was unhappy about something.

A short while later, back at the barn, Henry and

Tom caught up with Alec just as Alec finished brushing out the Black's mane. Henry was holding a copy of the sports section from the morning's newspaper between two fingers, looking at it as if it were a squashed cockroach he just found behind a water bucket.

Henry handed Alec the newspaper and folded it back to an article titled "The Big Four at Fairfield."

"Read it," Henry said.

"Beauty Pageant," read the caption beneath an old photo of the Black standing in the winner's circle at Belmont back in New York. Alec scanned the article as he walked the stallion down the shed row to his stall. "Irish race fans will get their first good look at this legendary runner in the flesh," it said, then noted that many local trainers maintained the Black to be "over-the-hill, over-rated and under-raced."

Alec handed the newspaper back to Tom, who shook his head with exaggerated indignation. Tom turned to Henry. "Such impudence," he said, "the cheeky whelps. 'Tis no way to treat someone far from home."

Alec couldn't tell if Tom was being serious or just trying to get a rise out of Henry. The old trainer grumbled something under his breath. Tom put his arm around Henry and then gave him a slap on the back.

"Ah, don't take it to heart, Henry. You're in Ireland

now, land of the wink and the nod. 'Tis just publicity. Read between the lines."

Henry gave an indignant snort. "I am reading between the lines. And over and under the lines," he said. "I know when we're being insulted."

Tom laughed. "You're surprised?" he said. "The American press says the same thing about our horses when we fly them to the States. The plain truth is that your American-bred horses generally run better at American tracks while our European horses do better on our own turf. Look at the odds on the last bunch that we shipped over to your Breeders' Cup. Good horses they were too, champions all. Not a one of them went off at better than ten to one."

Henry snorted. "None of them placed in the money either."

"My point exactly," Tom said. "And I can't remember the last time one of your horses shipped over here and did much better. You can't be too shocked when our local scribes point that out. The Black might be a big hero in the States, but he has never raced in Ireland and has never proven himself on European grass."

"Why, the Black is twice the horse of any—"

"Sure he is," Tom interrupted. "By the saints, cousin, you weren't born yesterday. You know the papers are just trying to drum up business." He jabbed at the newspaper with his finger. "Anyhow, it should make for a nice crowd here tomorrow. You know that's what this nonsense in the paper is about as well as I do. A little controversy just spices things up. We'll see how it plays out for the race."

the foster stakes

A SHIVER RAN up Alec's spine as he walked out the door of the jockeys' locker room. He wasn't nervous really, just a bit cold, and his lightweight jockey silks weren't helping matters much. He rubbed the palms of his hands together, cupping them to his lips to blow some warmth into his fingers. At least the air was dry, he thought. The rain that was forecast to wet the track last night never materialized. There had been some clouds in the morning, but now the sky was sunny and clear.

Alec followed the Black and Henry to the paddock and the saddling stalls. Henry cinched up the girth strap on the sliver of leather that was the Black's racing saddle and then leaned in close to Alec.

"Remember what Tom was saying about the turf out there," Henry said. "Rain or no rain, it's softer than the Black's used to."

"He'll take to it fine," Alec said.

"I think you're right. Just don't let him have his head too early."

Alec nodded. "I'll do what I do, Henry. Like always."

Henry gave Alec a sly smile. "Not to worry, kid. The Black looks great, as relaxed as I've ever seen him. I think he just might give the local doubters a little surprise today."

Alec looked up at his horse. The Black did look magnificent standing there, head held high, the sunlight sparkling in his dark eyes, his coat rubbed to a fine velvet luster.

"I guess this Irish weather agrees with him," Alec said.

"I'm feeling lucky today, son," Henry said. "Just remember to keep an eye on that mare. She's a classic closer and will be there at the end. But I still don't think she can stay with the Black. I saw her run at Belmont last year. She didn't even hit the board."

"We're not in the States anymore," Alec said quietly. "This is her home turf. Things might be different here."

Henry touched his old fedora for luck, shook his head and smiled. "Not that much different," he said quietly.

Despite the partisan comments in the newspapers

about American racehorses in general and the Black in particular, plenty of people lined the paddock to watch the Black being saddled for the big event, his first trip on Irish grass. Like at any track anywhere, the crowd was an odd mix of young and old, rich and poor. All were there to cheer on their favorites. They'd staked their bets—some would win, most would lose, all seemed to appreciate that the meeting of these champions from around the world was something special.

Alec looked around him as the horses filed out into the walking ring for the post parade. There was the big gray stallion Kinsman from Australia who'd been winning races all over Europe that year. Behind him stood the fiery red Tamerlaine from France, another legendary runner and sire. As a three-year-old, the compact dark bay Izvestero from Argentina was younger than the rest and also just coming off a successful campaign in South America. Like the Black, all three horses had been flown in especially for this event. All were champions in their own right, having earned millions of dollars in winnings among them.

The hometown hero, and favorite with the bettors, was the Irish-bred Jinga Jean, a big, heavyset mare with a light chestnut–colored coat. Her entry in the feature race was far from a novelty presence. She'd proved herself running with the boys, winning more often than not, and held the honor of having set more track records in Ireland than any filly or mare in history.

The paddock judge called riders up and Henry gave Alec a boost into the saddle. Soon Alec and the Black were following the other runners and their jockeys under the stands and out onto the track. The Black walked, jogged, then cantered easily up the track a ways, then turned and headed back to the start.

"I'm with you, Big Black," cried a tall, dark man standing by the rail, long dreadlocks trailing out from under his beehive-shaped cap like a nest of snakes.

"Take it home, Yank," howled a little old lady in the front row of the crowd.

"Yeah, take it all the way home," cried someone else. "All the way. And don't forget to be taking that Black devil with ye." Alec ignored the catcalls and kept his mind on the business at hand.

At two miles, the Foster Stakes was a long race, at least by American standards. That fact didn't worry Alec in the slightest. The Black could run farther and faster than any horse in the world when he wanted to.

The horses loaded into the gate without fuss. A moment later the doors flew open and the race was on. The Black got away well and found room to run, quickly striding into an easy gallop. Alec drew strength from the calm, confident feel of his horse beneath him.

There was only one way to ride a horse like the Black, Alec knew, and that was to let him run his own race in his own time. At this point Alec's job was to do one thing and one thing only—stay out of his horse's way. Crouching forward, he listened to the Black speak to him with his movements. The only parts of Alec's body touching the stallion were his hands, the calves of his legs and the inside of his feet.

They had plenty of time, so Alec looked around him as the Black settled close to the back of the pack. They were running well off the rail with five horses in front of them, positioned just ahead of Jinga Jean and behind Kinsman. As the horses made their first pass by the stands, Tamerlaine, the flame-colored French horse, took the initiative and went to the front. Alec glanced to his right and saw Jinga Jean run up beside the Black. She looked relaxed, as if she knew she had all the time in the world.

Alec watched the mare out of the corner of his eye. The Irish-bred favorite was certainly impressive, like a well-muscled ballet dancer. Watching her powerful forelegs swallow up the grass in front of her, Alec understood why Henry had warned him about her before the race.

In front of the pack, Tamerlaine had two lengths on the closest challenger for the early lead. The horses bunched up and rounded the first turn. Jinga Jean drifted back as Alec leaned into the turn, and he lost sight of her.

With his stride lengthening, the Black began picking off one runner and then another in front of him. Alec, his heels down, kept his weight centered in the middle of his horse, balanced so he barely moved. Relentlessly the Black edged through the pack, ears pricked, Alec crouching up into a cannonball on his back.

The Black switched strides, leading with his left front leg now and pulling for his head. Alec kept a firm grip on the reins. "Easy now," he whispered to his horse. "Plenty of time. That's it. Plenty of time."

As the other horses jostled for position along the backstretch, the Black switched leads again, a transition so practiced and smooth that Alec barely felt it. Approaching the far turn the runners began to bunch up. To either side Alec could hear jockeys talking to their horses, urging them on, or calling to each other for more racing room.

The stampede of horses swept through the turn and started down the homestretch. A gap began to separate two sets of runners from the front. In the lead, Izvestero, Tamerlaine and Kinsman were running head to head. A length behind them, Jinga Jean and the Black were pacing each other again, both running easy and well within themselves. Alec couldn't see it but just behind them a long-legged bay, an English-bred long shot named Effington Effect, was moving through the middle of the pack, now breaking free to challenge the leaders.

A roar of sounds swelled in Alec's ears, pounding hooves and the rush of wind. Alec flattened himself against his horse's neck, moving with the rhythm of the Black's mighty strides, beginning to urge his horse on now, digging in and keeping his focus well up the track.

They raced into the final furlongs and the gathering storm of noise from the crowd soon drowned out everything else. The wall of noise swelled in intensity, pushing the horses ever faster.

To one side, Alec saw the jockey riding the English-bred bay begin to make his bid, waving his whip and inching along on the outside of the Black. Alec eased the Black away from the bay, dropping closer to the rail. The colt Izvestero was tiring fast a few lengths ahead of him and falling back from the two front-runners. But instead of giving up, the Argentine's jockey now began pumping his arms, lifting Izvestero's head and urging the colt to hold on.

And then, suddenly, Izvestero bobbled a step. His forelegs buckled and he practically went down to his knees. The jockey flew forward, thrown high up onto

Izvestero's neck. Somehow the colt recovered himself and didn't go down. His jockey skillfully regained his seat and kept on riding.

It was an incredible lucky break for them but too late to help Alec and the Black, who were coming up fast behind Izvestero. When Alec saw the colt stumble, he knew immediately that there wouldn't be enough time to pull up before colliding into Izvestero's hindquarters.

Facing a jockey's worst nightmare, Alec did what he had to do. He took a chance. If there was no room in front of them, they would find room somewhere else. As if by telepathy, Alec and the Black moved toward the same decision at the exact same time. The Black gathered himself and jumped up and over Izvestero's rump.

Some people who were there that day said they'd never seen anything like it. Others said it wasn't really a jump over the colt, but more like a hop to the side. Hop or jump, the result was that the Black barely avoided ramming Izvestero, somehow managing to land his flight through the air with hardly a break in stride or missed step.

But Alec had no time to appreciate his luck. Izvestero wasn't the only horse on the track with the Black that day. All Alec knew was what was right in front of him, and suddenly it wasn't Izvestero any longer. It was Jinga Jean.

The Black swung sideways just as the mare's rider edged to the outside a notch, giving the stallion a few more inches of precious running room. But it wasn't quite enough to keep from bumping up alongside Jinga Jean. It wasn't a hard hit, but immediately Alec knew it would mean trouble with the officials. Better a bump from the side than risking a pileup on the rail, he thought.

For her part, the bump only caused Jinga Jean to change leads and come on stronger. Up front, Effington Effect was making his bid for the lead. Both Tamerlaine and Kinsman were fading fast. Into the final furlong, it was a three-way race between the Black, Jinga Jean and Effington Effect, the long shot desperately trying to fend off the late charge of the two closers, Jinga Jean and the Black.

No one questioned the fact that if the race had been another sixteenth of a mile longer, the Black would clearly have won it. As it was, he blew past Effington Effect and caught Jinga Jean just at the wire for a photo finish. At least that was the way Alec saw it.

Alec slapped the Black's neck warmly. It was close, but he felt sure the Black got a nose in front at the end. He glanced to his left and saw Jinga Jean's rider claiming victory by pumping his fist in the air.

The Black eased up, shortening his great, gliding

strides. "Good boy," Alec said to his horse. "You showed 'em. That's my guy."

Leaning back in his saddle, Alec slowed the stallion to a walk. The Black held his head thrust out, tossing his mane and bouncing slightly as Alec turned him around and they headed back to the stands.

It was then that Alec noticed it. Something was off, a barely perceptible tick in the Black's stride. There it was again. Immediately Alec dismounted and knelt down next to the Black's left hind leg. The Black flinched visibly and pulled away as Alec ran his hand down the stallion's cannon bone.

The breath caught in Alec's throat. Must have been that jump, he thought. Maybe the landing wasn't as smooth as it seemed.

Alec steadied the Black, then walked the stallion a few paces, watching the action of the stallion's hooves, seeing the slight limp in the left hind leg that was plainly visible now.

Not too serious, Alec told himself. Probably just a slight sprain. Sure, that was all it was. Another voice in his head said there was no telling what the trouble was, not just yet.

Alec walked the Black back to his barn, the stallion's limp more pronounced now that the race was over and the rush of excitement was starting to wear off. Spectators were crowding the walking path. Alec saw Henry and Tom push their way through the crowd and duck under the railing. Tom walked a few strides in front of the Black, calling "Make way" and "Horse walking here."

"Easy, boy," Alec said as he ran his hands over his horse's neck. "Easy now."

Henry caught up with Alec and took his arm. "What happened?"

Alec shook his head. "I don't know. I'm hoping it's just a sprain."

Even with his limp, the Black was hot and needed to cool out before he went into his stall. Alec led the stallion to the walking path beside the barn so the Black could walk off some of the race.

Henry and Tom tagged along with Alec as he led the Black around the path. "I still don't know how it happened," Alec said. "The Black landed that jump like a pro steeplechaser. I barely felt anything."

"From where we were in the stands, it was hard to tell what happened," Henry said. "We were standing behind some fool who suddenly decided to climb up onto his seat the last furlong."

"The horse in front of me bobbled and almost went down," Alec explained. "The Black had to jump out of the way at a full gallop." He shook his head. "Then we bumped into the filly. It was a wild ride, I'm telling you. We're lucky we didn't pile up."

Alec stopped the Black a moment, knelt down and ran his hand lightly over the tender spot of the Black's leg. Through his fingertips he could feel the heat swelling the muscle. Maybe nothing, he thought. Maybe. He stood up again and rubbed the Black's neck.

"Let's get some ice on it," Henry said.

INTO THE WEST

WHEN HE FINALLY learned the results of the race, Alec wasn't surprised to hear the officials had decided to disqualify the Black for interference. They gave the race to Jinga Jean, followed by Effington Effect and Tamerlaine. To Alec, the results were unimportant. All that mattered to him was the Black's health.

The swelling around the cannon bone was worse when Alec felt the Black's leg the next morning. After the stallion ate his breakfast, Alec took him for a walk around the shed row. They were in the wash bay a few minutes later when Henry and Tom Dailey brought the X-rays and sound scans back from the lab.

"Nothing here," Henry said. "Just a sprain, I guess."

Alec dried his hands and looked over the X-ray chart. Everything looked normal—at least there were no fractures of any sort. He gave a sigh of relief.

"We were lucky," Alec said. "Anyhow, we still better keep an eye on him."

"We sure will," Henry said.

Alec stepped into the wash bay again. The Black stood still as he ran the water from the hose over the stallion's back and legs.

"And I'll tell you something else," Alec said. "Right now the idea of that plane ride back to the States doesn't thrill me any. You know how the Black is. He's not the greatest traveler on the best of days. The last thing he needs to be doing is banging around in a box stall for an eight-hour plane ride over the Atlantic."

Henry shook his head. He had already been talking that morning about catching an early plane back to New York. "Home is the best place for him now."

Tom smiled. "Not so fast, old man," he said. "Not so fast. Let's think this through. Do you mean to tell me that you're going to miss a visit to the ancestral home just because of a pulled muscle? Bring the Black and the lad and come out to the west with me for a few days. It'll be a grand time. We can have the Black there in a matter of hours, walk him in the cool salt water of the Atlantic. Nothing better to treat a sore leg than that. Certainly better than eight hours in a plane plus another long van ride up to Hopeful Farm."

Henry frowned. "Tourism is about the last thing on my mind right now."

"Tourism?" Tom laughed and gave Henry a warm clap on the back. "I'm talking about water therapy, Henry. Why, a few days by the sea will do you all some good. Besides, I want you to meet Calypso."

"Who?" Henry asked.

"You know," Tom said, "my colt. The one I wrote you about."

Henry and Tom bantered back and forth. Finally Henry shrugged and glanced at Alec. "It's up to you, Alec," he said.

Alec wasn't sure what to think. The Black no longer flinched when Alec felt his leg, but the heat was still there, and so was the swelling. Alec looked at the Black, trying to read his horse's mood. Despite the fact that he favored his right rear leg, he seemed frisky enough, playing with the sponge as Alec ran it down between his eyes and across his nose.

"I guess there is no reason to rush things," Alec said after a minute. "Let's go with Tom. I'm in no hurry to get back in an airplane and I doubt the Black is either. Besides, we planned to be here a few more days, didn't we? If we try leaving earlier we'll have to change plane reservations, and you know how tough that can be."

Henry nodded. "True enough," he said.

"'Tis settled, then," Tom said. "I'll take care of everything. Don't worry about a thing." He glanced up at the Black, who tossed his head, looking bored, wet and anxious to get going, no matter where. Tom rubbed his hands together and smiled. His eyes sparkled. "Why, the seaside at Oorloch is the best medicine you could ask for. Let's start packing up so we can get started. I don't want to get caught in the afternoon traffic if I can help it."

They walked the Black so he could dry off. Then, after a light grooming, the Black's legs were carefully rebandaged and he was loaded in Tom's van. Alec rode in the back with his horse.

Soon they were leaving the suburbs of Dublin behind. They drove past the low-lying Midlands, north and then west to the towns Westmeath, Longford and Boyle. In between the towns were pristine pastures bordered with stone walls. Water was everywhere— rivers, lakes and streams, ditches, gullies and backwaters.

The weather began to change. Damp air misted the inside of the windshield and Tom wiped off the condensation with his shirtsleeve. Outside, gray clouds scattered across the sky. Alec could see low walls of stone crisscrossing green meadows and rolling hills. Beyond that he saw sheep smudged with blue dye grazing in a field. And something else caught Alec's eye as well, something from another time altogether. Parked along the side of the road was an old-fashioned trailer, about the size of a small room, complete with a little chimney tilting up from the roof. Hitched to the front of the trailer were two big muscled cart horses.

"That's something you don't see every day," Henry said when he saw the horse cart.

"Travelers," Tom said, waving a hello out the window as they passed.

"Are they like the Amish people who don't believe in cars?" Alec asked.

"Not really," Tom said. "They're Irish gypsies, nomads who've been wandering this land since pre-Christian Celtic times. Most pull their trailers with cars these days, but a few still follow the old ways and use cart horses. You'll see caravans like that one on the back roads from time to time."

"What are they like?" Alec asked. "How do they live?"

"Some deal in scrap metal and car parts. Others are craftspeople, peddlers, antiques dealers or fortune-tellers. Still others are on the dole. But whatever they do for a living, no self-respecting Traveler would sell his time for wages or live his life working on someone else's schedule. Freedom is everything to them. Travelers believe it's not healthy to be shut inside four walls with no trees in sight. They'll sleep in a stable before sleeping in a house."

"I feel that way myself sometimes," Alec said.

Henry grunted. "You're young," he said. "You'll learn to appreciate a soft bed when you reach my age."

Tom shook his head. "It's a hard life. The open spaces are drying up. There are more and more regulations on where they may camp and where they may not. Sometimes there are conflicts with the settled communities and the police. Mrs. Pierce, the woman who keeps house for me, has some Traveler blood in her," Tom said. "You'll meet her soon enough. She can tell you all about the Travelers."

Out the window Alec saw a man in a wool cap who was tilling a field. "Probably hoeing potatoes," Tom said.

"By hand?" Alec asked. "Farmers till their fields by hand here?"

"Some of them," Tom said.

Alec thought how unlikely it would be to see a horse-drawn trailer or a farmer working his fields by hand back home in the States. Driving through the countryside here was like driving back in time.

The horse van continued west and soon Alec saw a road sign announcing that they were approaching their destination, County Sligo. The sign was printed in Irish with an English translation below it. "We're almost home now," Tom said.

They passed a clear stream, more potato fields and stone walls. Stunted, windswept trees dotted the low green hills as they neared the coast. The weather turned gloomy. The road began to twist and turn. It dipped, and before it started climbing again, Alec could hear the roar of the waves.

"Ah, the sound of the sea," Tom said. " 'Tis music to the ears."

"Did Alec tell you his sea-horse story, Tom?" Henry asked, a hint of sarcasm in his voice. "What do you call it again, a sharpie?"

"Kelpie," Alec corrected.

"Yes, he told me a bit," Tom said.

"Henry thinks I'm crazy," Alec said.

"If so, you are not the only one," Tom said. He laughed his good-natured laugh. "We Irish can be a superstitious lot." Henry shook his head.

At last Tom turned the horse van down the main street of Oorloch, an isolated fishing village by the sea. They drove through the town, passing ordered houses of cut stone with window boxes of flowers in summer bloom. Brightly painted shops crowded along the high streets above the harbor.

On the other side of Oorloch the road led through green fields again. Sheep and cattle grazed contentedly. Isolated white sandy roads ran off to the sea. A faint smoky scent blew in through the open windows. "Smell that, lad?" he said. " 'Tis peat. Burning peat. Nothing else smells quite like an Irish turf fire." Tom smiled broadly, stuck his head out the window and inhaled deeply. To Alec the burning turf smelled sort of sweet, like molasses or pipe tobacco mixed with the smell of burning grass.

Tom brought his big head back inside the window again. "Peat's what everyone used to heat their houses in the old days," Tom said. "We don't have the coal they do in England—one reason for the lack of factories and heavy industry here in Ireland. Plenty of grass, though. Some of the finest in the world, I reckon."

The van edged off the road slightly as Tom was talking and waving his hands around, pointing out the sights. "Just watch the road, cousin," Henry said, then jerked his thumb toward the back of the van. "This isn't one of your old plow ponies riding back there." Tom just laughed and shook his head.

They followed a lane along the top of a cliff to a green hump of land above a steep fall into the sea. At the very end of the lane was an old-fashioned cut-stone farmhouse with a barn and stables alongside. The house sat so close to the edge of the cliff that one wing seemed to be in imminent danger of crashing into the ocean below.

Tom pulled the van to a stop. Alec carefully walked the Black down the ramp, then turned him loose in an empty pasture to one side of the barn. The

Black made a slow lap along the fence. After the stallion turned his attention to grazing the green Irish grass, Alec and Henry followed Tom to the house and up the porch steps. Alec set his suitcase down as Tom fished in his pocket for the key.

It was a big, low-ceilinged dwelling lit by soft lights. The house seemed a little empty for just one person, Alec thought. Tom was a widower whose children had grown up and moved to the city. His only help around the house was Mrs. Pierce, a local woman who came in every few days to cook and clean.

Tom directed them to the living room, where a fire burned in a stone hearth. "Mrs. Pierce must have just left," he said. Alec warmed his hands by the fire and watched the play of firelight on the room. Above the crackle of flames he heard a clinking sound coming from the kitchen. Soon Tom appeared with a tray bearing three mugs of hot tea and a plate of warm rolls. They ate and drank. Before long Henry was dozing in a chair.

Alec went to check on the Black and bring him in for the evening. With the wind from the ocean, there was a chill in the air and Alec was glad to see the barn was warm and dry. As the Black ate his dinner oats, Alec walked up the aisle to see the rest of the barn.

The Black had one entire wing of the barn all to

himself. Stabled in the other wing were six Irish hunters, big horses known for their reliability and gentle
temperaments, sure-footed animals with muscular
frames and watchful eyes. Tom had said that he rented
these out to a nearby guesthouse that offered horseback tours of the area.

Alongside the hunters was a stable pony Tom
called Quackers and a two-year-old Thoroughbred
colt in training named Calypso, the colt that Tom had
talked up in his letters to Henry. As Alec watched
Calypso, he knew why Tom held such high hopes for
him. The colt's well-defined lines, his long limbs and
powerful hindquarters, testified to his good breeding.
He wasn't an overly large horse yet, Alec thought, but
as a two-year-old he still had room to grow.

Alec returned to the other side of the barn. The
Black had finished eating and hung his head over the
open half door. His eyes were starting to look sleepy.
Alec stayed with his horse awhile and then meandered
down the barn aisle to the door. Outside, the sun was
just setting in the west. He decided to go for a walk
and take a quick look around. It would feel good to
stretch his legs after the long van ride here from the
track.

A breeze rustled the tall grass along the fence as
Alec started up the driveway toward the lane. The taste
of salt from the Atlantic was thick in the air. High

above, seagulls romped in the wind. To the left, beyond the dunes, was the sea. To the right was a
heather-colored landscape of fields. Sheep sheltered
themselves from the wind behind the crumbling walls
of an ancient stone dike. A fine drizzle began to fall,
but not enough to make him want to return to the
house.

Except for the surf and a faint sigh of wind, the silence all around was absolute. The quiet hovered in
the air. To Alec it felt like a conscious, living presence,
nonhuman yet somehow very, very real. He climbed
atop one of the low dunes and looked down to the
mist-shrouded waterline. Again he sensed the strange,
nonhuman presence lingering in the quiet. For a moment he thought he saw something moving wraithlike
in and out of the fog down by the water's edge. But
surely it was only shifting shadows and wisps of mist.

Turning up his jacket collar against the wind, Alec
climbed down the back side of the dune and started
off to the house. Hurrying along, he couldn't deny the
uneasy feeling creeping over him. It was as if he was
being watched.

6

IRISh SANDS

ALEC FOUND TOM and Henry already eating dinner at the kitchen table. "Here he is," Tom said as
Alec walked in. "We were wondering where you were
off to."

Alec slid back his chair and sat down to join them.
"Took a little stroll down to the beach," he said. "It's
really quite beautiful. I think I understand why you
like this place so much. I think the Black likes it too."

Tom smiled with pride. "Aye, lad. The Irish grass.
The sea air. There's nothing like it. The beaches around
Oorloch are some of the finest in all Ireland. And the
least visited. You can walk for miles sometimes and
not see a solitary soul."

"I don't know if long walks are on the program
for the Black right now," Henry said.

"Believe me," Tom said. "Even a short walk in the
shallows will do wonders for him. Now find a bowl
and help yourself to some of the lovely lamb stew Mrs.

Pierce made for us. She is a wonder in the kitchen, that one. Certainly I could manage the housekeeping here by myself. But as to her cooking, I don't think I could live without that."

With one mouthful of the delicious stew, Alec knew what Tom was talking about. Alec hadn't thought he was very hungry, but once he tasted the delicious mix of lamb, cabbage, onions, carrots and peas in gravy, his appetite returned. Two and a half servings later he washed the last bite down with a tall glass of bitter lemon soda, so different from the all-too-sweet American-style soda.

After they'd cleared the table and cleaned the dishes, Henry and Tom retired to the living room. Tom switched on the TV and turned to a news channel to check on the local weather forecast. Pocketing a carrot from the refrigerator, Alec walked out to the barn to check on the Black and see how he was faring in his new surroundings.

Alec opened the barn door and started down the aisle. The only sign of life was the soft, sleepy sounds of the horses rustling in their stalls. The air was scented with the familiar barn smells of hay and ammonia. Most of the horses seemed to be snoozing, but the pony Quackers poked his head over the open half door of his stall as Alec walked by.

"What's this, then?" Alec said, trying to imitate

Tom's gentle Irish brogue. He gave Quackers a pat on the neck, then pulled a piece of carrot from his pocket and waved it under the horse's nose. With a quick bob of the head, the pony whinnied, then took the carrot in his teeth and began chomping away loudly. "Shh," Alec said. "You'll wake everybody up. I only brought one carrot and that's not enough for everyone."

Alec kept company with Quackers as he ate, then walked down the aisle and across to the Black's stall on the other side of the barn. Slipping the latch on the screened-in top half of the stall door, he stepped inside. The stallion was half dozing and snuffled sleepily as Alec moved closer. "Good boy," Alec said. "All settled in for the night? That's a boy."

Alec stayed with his horse, speaking to him softly, rambling on about nothing in particular, only trying to comfort the Black with the sound of his voice, the words unimportant so long as they were familiar and gentle. After a few minutes, he closed up the barn again and stepped out into the starry night.

Everyone was up early the next morning and out to the barn. First thing, Alec checked the Black's injured leg. There was still a little heat there, and some swelling too, but the good news was that it didn't seem to trouble the stallion's appetite. The Black ate with gusto, cleaning his feed trough down to the last grain.

Tom introduced Alec and Henry to Bartley, a

retired jockey who managed the barn and helped look after Tom's horses. The man was small but athletically built and looked to be somewhere in his mid-thirties. His eyes sparkled as he gave Alec a big smile and they shook hands.

"A pleasure to meet you," Bartley said. "I've been looking forward to seeing your horse in the flesh." Alec brought the Black out of his stall. Bartley whistled softly. "He looks fierce like one I used to know," he said. "Horse that shipped over from Spain named El Dorado."

Tom gave Alec a downward nod of the chin and a huge wink. "Why doesn't that surprise me?" Tom said. "Bartley here has saddled as many horses as anyone in Ireland."

"Not too many horses anywhere like this one, son," Henry said.

"I'll give you that, sir," Bartley said, his eyes saying he meant it.

They fed Quackers and the hunters, and while the horses ate, Tom invited everyone back to the house for a quick breakfast. Alec was anxious to get down to the beach. He'd barely sat down before he was up and out the door, headed for the barn again, leaving Bartley, Tom and Henry to fight over the sports section of the newspaper.

The Black touched Alec's chest with his nose and

gave him a little shove when Alec opened his stall door. "So it's like that, is it?" Alec said. "Don't you want to go for a walk?" Reaching up, Alec slipped a web halter over the stallion's head, buckled it and clipped on a short rope. The Black perked up as they walked outside, and a minute later Alec was leading the Black down the lane and through the front gate.

An offshore wind blew in from the east, soft and quiet and so different from the gusty sea breezes that swept in from the whitecapped Atlantic the evening before. As they walked along, Alec noticed a big, shiny black cat sunning himself atop one of the ruined stone walls lining the lane.

The old lane took them down to where he could feel the wet from the ocean. Again Alec whiffed the musty smell of burning turf. Morning light bathed the tips of the dunes in gold. Beyond them the beach stretched on for miles, ending at Oorloch to one side and a distant point to the other. Seagulls played in the wind, spiraling up, swooping down and loitering in groups along the beach. Alec turned around a moment and saw another black cat watching from atop one of the dunes. Or perhaps, Alec thought, it was the same one he'd seen earlier. Perhaps it was following him. Strange to see a cat at the beach, Alec thought, though this one seemed quite at home here.

They walked to the water's edge and then moved into the shallows, the Black wading in the cool water up to his knees and hocks. Alec found a nice level area where the water was only a foot deep. It wasn't always easy for him to keep pace with the long-striding stallion. His pants were rolled up as far as they'd go but they were soon wet up to his thighs.

The water temperature was chilly but not really cold, Alec thought. Anyway, the Black seemed to like it and nickered softly as they sloshed through the shallows together. There were not even any flies to bother them.

A gentle breeze smoothed the surface of the long swells breaking on a sandbar just offshore. The foam from the broken waves rolled in crumbling white lines to the shallows and washed up onto the beach, crackling and fizzling out in the sand.

Suddenly Alec glimpsed a dark shape moving inside the wall of an approaching wave. Was it a dolphin? A shark? But when it broke the surface, Alec saw that it was a seal, a creature about the size of a large dog. The seal dove, then quickly surfaced again, looked around the bay, then turned his dark brown face to gaze toward Alec and the Black. After a moment he ducked underwater again to vanish as quickly as he'd appeared.

The Black gave a snort and pawed the water. "None of that now," Alec said. "That guy lives here. We're just his guests. Behave." Tossing his head, the Black gave a shrill whistle, then bucked and bounced until Alec could get him settled down again.

Alec led the Black up onto the dry sand and looked around. Sea and sky seemed to go on forever here, and it was easy to pretend they were on a desert island somewhere, that there were no other people anywhere, no houses behind the dunes or beyond the cliffs. Then, as he walked along, Alec glimpsed something up ahead, something that told him he was not alone. Just at the tidemark were the remains of a sand castle. Beside it was a drawing, the outline of a running horse, studded with white shells.

Alec pulled the Black to a stop to take a closer look. The twenty-foot image of the horse was large but well-balanced, the head small and wedge-shaped. The long, sweeping lines of the horse's legs reached all the way down to the water's edge. The Black whiffed at the strands of seaweed that were fashioned artfully into the horse's mane and tail.

Who did this? Alec wondered as he circled around the horse figure. The shells were all pearly white except for one colored shell, a blue-green circular spiral that represented the horse's eye. Alec reached down and picked it up. It shone like green ice in his hand

and was smooth to the touch, as if covered with jade enamel.

As Alec leaned closer he realized he'd never seen another shell quite like it before. He turned the thing over in his hand and looked again. The spiral pattern on the underside of the shell caught the early-morning light, sparkling and flashing the sunlight back into his eyes in the most hypnotic way. It was as if the shell was alive somehow, an eye staring back at him. Alec rubbed the shell dry on his jeans and put it into his pocket. Suddenly he wished he'd brought a camera so he could take a picture of the sand horse before it disappeared.

Again he wondered who might be responsible for the drawing. Whoever it was, there certainly didn't seem to be anyone here now. There was not even a footprint in the sand. The shore break on the incoming tide surged up the beach and took a swipe at the sand horse's hooves. It was sort of sad, Alec thought. Before long there would be nothing left, like the sand castle now melting into the sea.

With one last look at the horse figure, Alec pointed the Black up the beach. Soon they were off again, slowly splashing through the shallows. They rounded a bend in the beach. On the other side, Alec found what he was looking for. It was perfect for them, a shallow tide pool with a hard sand bottom, like a beachside swimming pool complete with a whirlpool bath at one end. Scrunching his toes in the sand, he enjoyed the soft touch of the circulating water as it washed in and out of the tide pool, pushed by the lazy pulse of the waves.

The sun was high over the dunes when Alec started thinking about turning around and going back. He wasn't wearing a watch but figured it must be past ten o'clock. He thought about continuing on but there wasn't a whole lot farther they could go anyway. The beach ended less than a mile up the way, where a steep cliff jutted down to a point of water-carved stone.

Before Alec had set out that morning, Tom had told him that the point of rocks at this end of the beach would not be passable due to the tide. According to Tom, the only way to keep going here was along the beach, as the sheer cliffs were too steep to climb. When the tide was low, it was possible to take your chances and pick your way through the exposed rocks, Tom said, but otherwise there was no way around the point, especially if there was any surf.

The Black stood with his ears pricked and head held high, very still, as if scenting something in the wind. "Come on, boy," Alec said, giving the lead line a little tug. "Let's get going."

Just as they turned around and started back to the farm, the silence was cut by a shrill cry. As unlikely as it seemed, the cry sounded like that of a horse, a stallion's challenge to battle.

The Black whirled and reared back, catching Alec off guard and jerking the lead line from Alec's grip. An instant later the Black was running off toward the point, bucking and twisting and snaking out his neck.

"Whoa, whoa," Alec cried out as he scrambled after him.

Something was moving between the scattered rocks bordering the point. It could have been anything, but after what Alec had heard, he could only assume it was a horse. The Black raced up the beach, shrilling loudly as he closed in on whatever it was that was there. He rushed all the way to the point, stopping only when the concentration of rocks made it impossible to go any farther.

The Black danced around at the water's edge a moment, then paced up and down the beach until Alec caught up with him. Alec scolded him for running off, and scolded himself for letting it happen. The Black continued to whinny but stood still now, staring out to the inaccessible rocks of the point.

Alec scanned the beach and quickly recognized some hoofprints in the sand that he was certain didn't belong to the Black. The hoofprints led down to the water's edge, but after that they vanished in the wet sand. Where was the passage through the rocks? Alec wondered. He looked closer and saw that, even with the incoming tide, there still might be enough exposed beach, in between waves, to make it around the point. If, Alec thought, you could run fast and time everything just right so as not to be caught by the waves. And if you were really lucky.

MORA

ON THE WAY back to the farm, Alec recalled that morning on Long Island a few weeks ago and the horse he had seen on the beach, the one that had appeared to vanish into the sea. That encounter had been strange enough, he thought, and now this. He turned and looked back toward the point. At least he'd seen hoofprints this time. And dodging the rocks in between waves could be a plausible explanation for how the horse was able to come and go. Yet somehow it just didn't seem possible, especially when he saw the near-constant crash of surf against the rocks now.

They rounded the bend in the beach and soon came to the place where he had found the drawing of the horse in the sand earlier. There was nothing there now, just waves washing over the beach. After what Alec had seen at the point, the horse drawing in the sand took on a whole new significance. Of just what, he wasn't quite sure.

Back at the farm, Alec turned the Black loose in a small, tree-lined pasture adjacent to the larger pasture shared by the rest of the horses. Soon the stallion set to munching grass in the shade. Alec leaned against the fence, watched his horse graze, and again thought about what had happened on the beach.

The porch door slammed up at the house and a minute later Tom came over to say hello. He wasn't too surprised when Alec mentioned the horse at the point.

"Maybe we should call around and see if anyone is missing a horse," Alec suggested.

"Oorloch is a small town," Tom said. "If that's the case, I'll hear about it. But I wouldn't worry too much. Whoever it was you saw on the beach, he's probably found his way home by now."

Alec nodded his head, quickly deciding that there was no point in making a big deal about the horse on the beach. It wasn't his business. Tom lived here and he didn't seem concerned. And Tom had other things on his mind. He was waiting for word about an upcoming race scheduled to be run at a track in England. The race card was full, but Tom was hoping for a last-minute scratch that might give him a chance to enter Calypso.

In the afternoon a horse van came to pick up four of the Irish hunters. They were being rented out for a four-day trail ride touring the towns of the neighboring countryside. Tom knew the guide and was confident the horses would be well cared for.

As the last horse was being loaded, Tom received a phone call, and when he came back outside he announced he'd just received the news he'd been hoping for. One of the English horses was pulling out of the race and the officials said there would be room for Tom's entry. He rubbed his hands together and smiled.

"This is it, lads," he said. "Over there they don't know me from Adam. With any luck we'll get off at terrific odds and score big." He turned to Alec. "I don't mean to be an inattentive host, but you understand, lad. This race, I just can't pass up. I should only be gone for a few days."

Alec nodded. "We'll be all right here. The Black likes the beach and Henry . . ."

"I was thinking of going with Tom, tell you the truth," Henry said. "We were talking about it earlier."

"You never were much for the life of the country gentleman," Alec said.

Henry shrugged. "Fact is," he said, "I'd like to see this colt of Tom's run. You and the Black seem to be adapting well enough here. You'll be all right."

"Sure they will," Tom said. "Bartley will be here and he can help you with anything that comes up around the farm. And Mrs. Pierce will be coming round as well. She'll take care of the house and your meals. You won't even know she is there. Just sit back, enjoy her home cooking and let the Black recover at his own pace. You'll both have a grand time."

The conversation quickly returned to Calypso's prospects in the upcoming race. Alec listened to the two Dailey men chatter about the race and felt a smile creep across his face. Look at these guys, he thought. The more he saw the two of them together, the more their differences seemed to fade and their similarities became apparent. Tom was squarely built and big. Henry was smaller, rounder and close to twice Tom's age. Tom was easygoing and spoke with a soft and musical Irish accent. Henry sounded like the assertive New Yorker he was, always ready to take up a challenge, sometimes a little too gruff and to the point for his own good.

And yet, Alec thought, there was this glint in the eye, the way they moved sometimes, a tilt of the head, a nod of the chin, things that told you that they were related even though they'd been brought up on opposite sides of the Atlantic. Maybe it was because, as different in size and temperament as they were, in the end they shared the same bloodlines, like big Man o' War and little Sea Biscuit, both champions despite their differences.

It took the rest of the afternoon to get Calypso

ready for his trip to the airport, to pack tack trunks and load the trailer. After waving off the van, Alec checked on the Black, then walked inside the barn, strangely quiet now with so many of the horses gone. Wandering back to the house, he quickly descended on a delicious-smelling chicken potpie Mrs. Pierce had left for him on the stove.

Soon darkness began to fall and Alec returned to the pasture to bring the Black in for the night. Back at the house again, he made himself comfortable on the couch and spent the rest of the evening reading his book and listening to the sounds of the wind and waves, finally dozing off into a deep sleep.

The next morning Alec was up at dawn and out to the barn. He dished up a light breakfast of oats from the feed bin and then took the bucket down to the Black's stall. The Black nickered as Alec walked up the aisle, looked eagerly over the stall door and stretched his nose out. Alec grabbed the twitching upper lip and laughed as the stallion wriggled free. As the Black ate, Alec gave the injured leg another quick inspection and was relieved to feel no sign of swelling or unusual heat there.

From up the driveway came the sound of a car puttering, and a minute later Bartley walked into the barn. "Hallo, lad," called the barn manager.

"Good morning," Alec called back. Bartley

immediately set to the task of getting the horses fed while the Black finished up his own breakfast.

Opening the stall door, Alec led the Black into the aisle to give him a quick going-over with a soft brush. As he swiped the brush over the stallion's coat, the Black leaned into each stroke, grunting with pleasure. Alec made the brushstrokes longer and stronger, enjoying them almost as much as the horse. He checked the stallion's legs and hooves, finding them all surprisingly clean.

Alec was extra cautious as he walked the Black down the lane toward the beach, keeping a firm hand on the lead line. He was still mad at himself for losing his hold on the Black's lead the day before. Letting the Black run off like that had been a stupid mistake.

Once on the beach, Alec watched the seagulls and other seabirds frolicking over the waves breaking out on the sandbar. As they walked along the water's edge, Alec saw ripples moving in the water just off the shoreline. Perhaps it's another seal, he thought at first. But as the shadowy object moved closer he realized it was larger than any seal. There was definitely something there, though, Alec thought. Somewhere a seagull cried out, faint and eerie.

Alec walked along the shore watching the dark shape below the surface just offshore. A V-shaped wake trailed off the thing's back as it came closer. Suddenly he realized that it wasn't one creature but a whole school of fish. The fish were grouped so tightly together as they swam along that they appeared to be one single mass, now blue above and silvery white below, all going the same direction. When a pair of diving gulls descended upon them, the leader took a sudden turn and in a flash the fish scattered and were gone.

Up the beach a black bird was hopping around and picking at something in the sand. It looked like a crow but was bigger than any crow Alec had ever seen. Alec came closer and the black bird sprang into the air, then circled back and came to rest only a few feet up the beach from where Alec and the Black were walking.

Could it be a raven? Alec wondered. The bird certainly didn't seem to be afraid of people, or horses either, for that matter. It seemed to be almost tame. After a moment the crow or raven or whatever it was gave a hoarse cry and took off again.

Alec walked closer and saw what the bird had been pecking at, the remains of an apple and a few carrots strewn about in the sand. Someone must have left them there as a treat for the gulls. The Black sniffed at the apples until Alec pulled him away.

They reached the bend in the beach, and when they came to the other side, they surprised a girl sitting in the sand. The girl jumped up when she saw them.

The Black whinnied loudly. Alec clamped a hand over the stallion's nose to keep him still. "Sorry," Alec called to the girl. "I didn't mean to startle you."

The Black danced in place as the girl stepped forward, her eyes flashing between Alec and the stallion. She looked to be about twelve or thirteen years old, with a skinny build and a suntanned face. Her hair was a dark bronze color and fell to her shoulders. Alec noticed a bunch of carrots in an open bag on the ground at the girl's feet. So did the Black.

"Are you here for him?" the girl asked, her eyes filled with suspicion.

"Excuse me?" Alec said, trying to hold the Black still. He turned the Black in a tight circle to settle him down.

"Are you here to take him away?"

"Take who away?"

"Silver."

Alec shook his head. "Who is Silver?"

"That silver-colored horse. He doesn't belong to you?"

"Not me," Alec said. He nodded to the Black. "We were just going for a walk on the beach. But

I think I did see a horse yesterday morning down by the next point. Are there stray horses running loose around here?"

The girl shrugged. "I don't know. I just saw the one. I've been bringing him carrots and apples and leaving them on the beach for him. He's been eating them."

Alec nodded. "Maybe, maybe not. I saw a bird treating himself to a salad up the beach a couple minutes ago."

"Oh, Silver is eating them, all right," she said. "I saw him. He's been showing up on the beach every morning since that big storm last week. I still haven't been able to get close enough to touch him yet. A couple days ago I managed to get within a few feet, but that was the best I could do."

"Well, be careful," Alec said.

"He wouldn't hurt me," the girl said. "He's not dangerous. Just a bit shy, is all."

"With some horses you can't tell until it's too late."

The girl nodded her head. "Sort of like people."

"True enough," Alec said. "Anyway, someone should try to find out who owns him." The Black kept his attention focused on the bag of carrots at the girl's feet. He snorted and nudged Alec's shoulder. Alec pushed back, leaning against his horse's neck.

"I asked a police officer in town and he hadn't heard anything. Neither had the lady at the post office."

"Well, let me know if I can help. My name is Alec Ramsay. This is the Black." The Black lowered his head, sniffing toward the girl's bag of carrots.

"My name is Medora," she said as they shook hands politely. "My friends call me Mora."

"I'll call you Mora, then," Alec said.

"Nice to meet you, Alec," Mora said.

"Pardon me for saying so, but you certainly don't sound like you come from around here. Your accent doesn't sound very Irish."

Mora smiled. "That's because I grew up in America. Mom's back in the States now. I've only been in Ireland a month. I'm living here with my dad for the summer."

As they talked, Mora explained how she learned to ride at a neighbor's stable back in Ohio. She hadn't been in Ireland long enough to meet anyone, much less find a place to go riding.

They talked a minute or two more, and then Mora said she had to be getting home. She picked up her shoulder bag and pulled out one of the carrots. "A present for your Mister Black," she said, handing it to Alec. "Can I give it to him?"

Alec shook his head. "Maybe some other time. Like I said before, with some horses it's better to keep your distance unless they know you. This fella can be one of the ones you have to watch out for."

"Really?" she said. "He sure doesn't look that way to me."

"Well, he is. Anyhow, I'm sure he'll appreciate the carrot. And he'll know where it came from. He's well aware I'm out of treats at the moment."

"See you, then," the girl said. "And keep an eye out for Silver."

"I will," Alec said. "I'll be around in the morning for the next few days. I'm still surprised no one seems to be missing him."

"Maybe whoever owns him doesn't know he's gone."

Alec shrugged. "Maybe," he said. "I'll let you know if I see anything."

"Me too," Mora said, and then waved goodbye.

Alec waved back and then led the Black down to their favorite tide pool for another hour of wave water therapy. She seems nice, Alec thought as he and the Black cooled their feet. And now at least he had an explanation for why the Black had acted up the previous morning. He had forgotten to ask, but surely Mora was the sand artist responsible for that shell-studded horse figure he saw on the beach yesterday as well.

SILVER

ALEC RETURNED TO the farm and turned the Black loose in his pasture. Bartley was down at the barn, on a tack trunk, mending a bridle. On a bench next to him was a pile of tack that needed cleaning.

"Any word from Tom yet?" Alec asked.

"He called just a few minutes ago," Bartley said, looking up from his work. "It seems that they made the flight in time and had Calypso settled in at the track well before dark."

"When is the race, anyway?" Alec asked.

"Not for a few more days," Bartley said. "Tom wanted to get there early to give the colt a bit of time to get adjusted to the place."

"That makes sense," Alec said, "especially with a young colt like Calypso."

Alec picked up a rag and lent a hand cleaning the tack. As they worked the leather with rags and saddle soap, the two jockeys compared notes on English racing, American racing, the different kinds of horses in Europe and the Americas, the different turf surfaces, types of race fans and, most of all, the tracks.

"The variety adds some interest to the game," Bartley said as they worked. "Our tracks are not nearly as uniform as yours are. We might have sharp turns, wide turns, runs up hills and down into valleys, all in a single race. I've always wondered why the races at American tracks are all run counterclockwise on the flats instead of clockwise. Sounds a bit boring to me."

"I think it has more to do with politics than anything," Alec said. "Early Americans wanted to do things as differently from things in England as they possibly could, including horse racing, so from the very beginning the standard became running to the left." Alec picked up another bridle and wiped it with the rag in his hand. "There were exceptions, though," he added. "My home track at Belmont Park ran clockwise races for years after it first opened in 1905. In fact, the great Man o' War won the Belmont Stakes running right-handed in 1920. I believe it was the last year, though. After that they switched to running left-handed like everyone else in the States."

"It's becoming more common here too," Bartley said. "I've raced both left-handed and right-handed. Not much difference, if you ask me. Adjusting to the different courses is a different story."

As they were talking, Alec heard the sound of a car puttering up the lane.

Bartley didn't look up from his work. "That'll be Mrs. Pierce, back from the market," he said. "She goes shopping Tuesdays as a rule."

Alec glanced over to see a little, square-shaped car roll to a stop at the end of the driveway. A stout, gray-haired woman in a loose-fitting black dress stepped out and began wrestling with grocery bags in the backseat. Alec put down his work and jogged over to ask if he could be of assistance.

The woman smiled. "Well, that's mighty kind of you," she said. "Nice to meet a young man with manners." A dog jumped out of the open car door behind her. He was a good-sized dog, especially to fit in such a small car, maybe part Irish wolfhound and part something else, Alec thought. The old hound gave Alec a sleepy stare but could not muster a bark.

"You must be young Ramsay from America. I'm Mrs. Pierce. Welcome to Ireland, lad."

"Pleased to meet you," Alec said. The stout woman started for the house and Alec followed. She walked slowly, and the hound even more slowly. They made their way up onto the porch. The hound slipped through the open door and followed them inside.

Mrs. Pierce led the way to the kitchen. "Set those bags down anywhere," she said, turning around to shoo the dog outside. There was a momentary stand-off as the dog paid no attention to her. Finally he lowered his head and did as he was told.

"Good boy," Mrs. Pierce said, closing the screen door behind him.

"Nice dog," Alec said.

"Has a mind of his own, he does. Like all of us. I don't like it when people tell me what to do either. But Martin can sit out on the porch a bit. I don't need him under my feet just now."

Alec followed Mrs. Pierce back into the kitchen again. "I'll be breading a fish for your dinner tonight," she said, "fresh off the boat." Alec said that sounded great. He found a plate of cold cuts in the refrigerator and made a sandwich as Mrs. Pierce set to putting the groceries away.

"Tom said you were part Traveler," Alec said between bites. "That must be a great life, living on the road, camping out and all. I love the outdoors."

"Sure. In good weather there is nothing finer," she said, her voice becoming testy. "Irish winters are another story. And you always have to keep moving. The cops and the settled people can make it hard on the Travelers if they want to. Times are better now than they used to be, in that regard. To be honest, I haven't lived the Traveling life since I was a little girl. Been settled close to forty years, right here in Oorloch. But tell me about yourself. What's it like living in America these days?"

Mrs. Pierce listened as Alec described his home at Hopeful Farm, his parents, Henry and the Black. After he finished his lunch, Alec walked out to the barn again.

Afternoons seemed to be a slow time around the Dailey barn, as they are at many horse farms. Alec walked up the aisle, past Quackers and the two hunters. He could hear the quiet barn sounds, the soft rustle of a horse shifting his weight from hoof to hoof, then the sound of someone else nosing around in an empty feed trough, a muzzle thumping against the wood bin.

Going outside again, Alec strolled up to the Black's pasture, where the stallion stood, head drooping, under the shade of a tree. Probably snoozing, Alec thought. He watched his horse a moment, considering an afternoon siesta himself, then decided to take a little trip up the road to Oorloch instead. He'd been here two days already, so it was about time.

The weather was cool and clear, the early clouds long since blown away. The light along the road was luminescent and pearly. In Oorloch he found a village of neat storefronts and streets peopled with working men and women. From almost any point in town you

could see the small harbor where the boats came in
with their catch every evening. The faint odor of fish
hung in the air, carried up from the harbor by the
wind.

In town everyone seemed to be busy and pur-
poseful except him. He bought an ice cream cone and
ate it and then found some postcards that he could
send to his folks back home. After that he followed a
road that led down to the harbor. A fishing trawler
was just pulling away from the dock. The roar of its
engine tapered off to a low throb as it moved out into
the bay.

Alec walked past lobster pots stacked in piles
on the pier. The fish smell was stronger here, mixed
with the smell of fuel oil and seaweed. He continued
along the wharf and then started home along the
beach.

The beach near town was almost as deserted as it
was in front of Tom's farm. No one was swimming or
strolling among the dunes or even out fishing. Maybe
it was too late in the day for catching fish, Alec
thought. Or too early. The wind had turned onshore
now and it was blowing whitecaps out to the horizon.

Nearing the farm, Alec climbed to the top of one
of the smaller dunes. He looked out to sea a moment
and was about to turn toward home when he saw

something in the distance. From his vantage point he could tell it was someone leading a gray pony along the shoreline and heading straight his way.

Alec climbed down the dune and out onto the beach again. It was Mora, he soon realized. It looked like she had caught her pony after all. The pony gave a friendly neigh as he waddled closer, and Alec had to laugh at himself. This was far from the horse he imagined when he heard that wild cry on the beach earlier, not some mighty stallion but a pony, deep and wide through the girth, with thick legs, a Roman nose and a long mane. His sand-dusted coat was a wild mix of light and dark gray, the color of a storm cloud. Burrs and a few strands of dry seaweed clung to his tangled mane and tail.

Could this really be the horse that made the shrill cry that he'd thought he'd heard yesterday morning, Alec asked himself, the challenge that startled him and caused the Black to bolt? It didn't seem possible, but there he was, the mystery horse from the beach.

Mora waved and walked up to where Alec was waiting. "I called to him and this time he walked right up to me," she said breathlessly. "All I had for a lead was this," she said, pointing to a short piece of weathered nylon rope looped around the pony's neck, the sort of line a small boat might use to tie up at a dock.

"He's sure not what I thought he'd looked like," Alec said. "What are you going to do with him?"

Mora caught her breath and then looked down at her feet. "That's just the thing. The fact is, um, I thought maybe you could help me out with him. I don't really know many people around here yet. And my dad . . ." Mora was getting flustered. She hopped from one foot to another. The pony watched Alec with his large dark eyes and then rubbed his head hard against Mora's shoulder, almost knocking her down.

"What I mean is," she blurted out finally, "do you think maybe he could stay with you and the Black at Mr. Dailey's farm until his owner shows up?"

Alec laughed. "I guess you will have to do something with him. It's going to be dark soon. I don't suppose he can spend the night in your backyard."

Mora shook her head. "Not likely."

"Come on, then," Alec said.

They walked back to the farm and turned the scruffy pony out into a paddock. The pony trotted over to the water trough to drink, sucking the water into his mouth in long drafts. Suddenly the pony threw back his head and whinnied loud enough to attract the attention of the Black, who was sunning himself in an adjacent pasture. Alec saw the stallion looking around sleepily, ears showing only mild curiosity in the newcomer. After a moment the Black lazily ambled toward them.

"I don't think there should be any serious problems between these two," Alec said, "but if there will be we are going to find out now."

The Black came to the fence at the edge of the pasture and stood there studying them. His eyes were fixed on the pony, and Alec was glad to see there was no sign of anger or aggression in the Black's body language. And yet the stallion's gaze was intense with curiosity, as if he'd never seen a pony quite like this before.

Alec left Mora with the pony and walked over to his horse. When he reached over the railing, the stallion flared his nostrils. Slowly the Black moved closer. "That's a good boy," Alec called. He let the stallion sniff his hands again. Lifting the Black's muzzle, Alec felt the warm, sweet breath blowing on his face.

All at once the Black pulled back. With a snort, he turned and broke away into a flying gallop, bolting for the opposite end of the pasture. He ran with his ears strained forward and head held high and didn't stop until he reached the far end of the pasture. The Black stood still a moment, then circled back toward Alec, finally lying down to roll in the grass.

Alec leaned against the fence and listened to his horse settling himself. After a minute he walked down to the barn to look around for Bartley. His car was gone, so Alec guessed he must be off somewhere. There was no sign of Mrs. Pierce up at the house either. Inside the barn, Alec lifted the lid to the feed bin, measured a couple scoops of oats into a black rubber pail and took it outside.

Mora was walking the pony in lazy circles around the paddock ring, letting the lead line hang loose. Alec watched as the pony bounced lightly along, marking time in his own rolling, waddling gait.

"He certainly seems easygoing enough," Alec said. "I guess your friend knows a good thing when he sees it."

The pony pulled up and sniffed at the pail of oats in Alec's hands. "Good boy," Alec said softly. Soon the pony was hungrily chomping the oats. As Alec watched the pony eat, he noticed a pair of small, crescent-shaped scars on the pony's neck.

Mora rubbed the pony's forehead. "Too bad he can't talk. I'm sure he'd have a story to tell."

"I'll say," Alec said. "For living in the wild, this boy looks in pretty good shape. Probably all those carrots and apples and other treats you've been feeding him."

Mora smiled. "I doubt it. More likely he's been raiding some local farmer's field."

"Or living on seaweed."

"Seaweed?"

"Sure," Alec said. "The Black did it once. So did I."

"Really?"

"It was a long time ago. I'll tell you the story sometime."

Mora made a sour face. "Seaweed, ugh."

"The Japanese eat it all the time," Alec said. "Haven't you ever had sushi or California rolls? That black stuff they wrap the rice in? That's dried seaweed."

"I suppose," Mora said. "Still sounds gross to me."

"Believe me, if you're hungry enough, you'll eat just about anything."

Mora shook her head. "If you say so."

"Better give him a bath," Alec said after the pony had eaten. He showed her to a place where she could wash the pony and then returned to the barn office. He picked up the phone and called Bartley's home phone number.

"Not a problem, lad," Bartley said after Alec explained the lost pony situation.

"I imagine it'll be just for a day or two," Alec said, "just until his owner claims him. He must belong to somebody. He's too nice an animal to have been abandoned."

"Plenty of room in the barn at the moment,"

Bartley said. "And that lot we have left in the barn now are all easygoers, like old retired pensioners. If Calypso were here it might be different. He can be a hothead, that one. I'll call Tom and clear it with him, but I suspect he'll go along."

Alec returned to where the pony was finishing up his bath, standing calmly as Mora flicked off the last of the water with the scraper. "That was Bartley on the phone," Alec said. "You're in luck. He's agreed to put your friend up for the time being."

Mora's face brightened. "Really?" she said. "What a relief."

Alec found a currycomb, brush and rub rag in the tack room and took them out to the paddock. After walking the pony in slow circles so he could dry off, Mora eagerly began going over the pony with the rag and the brush. Then she set to work on his head and neck with the comb, carefully pulling it through his mane, stopping every so often to pick at burrs tangled there.

The pony stood quietly under the soft hands moving over him. When Mora was satisfied the forelock and mane were tangle free, clean and clear of burrs, she set to work on the pony's tail. Alec watched her closely, half expecting the pony to lose patience with all the girl's attentions. But it was not to be. The pony remained still and steady, his eyes lit with curiosity and intelligence. He held his head high, his neck a proud arc under his short, light-colored mane, his coat shiny and smooth since his bath.

"So far so good," Alec said.

Mora smiled. "I think he might be a little tired."

Alec ran his hand over the pony's warm coat, surprisingly soft considering it appeared he'd been living on the beach. "I'll get a stall ready," Alec said. "You can bring him in then."

In an empty stall to one end of the barn, Alec spread a fresh layer of straw bedding over the floor, then prepared hay and water. When everything was ready he called Mora.

Alec kept a few feet ahead as Mora led the pony up the aisle toward his stall. The barn's few residents were already bedded down for the night. Over the half doors one of the Irish hunters turned his head from the hay net where he was munching a mouthful of timothy hay. He stopped eating and watched the pony pass down the barn aisle, his expression puzzled, his eyes wary.

Once the pony was settled in, Alec told Mora she should be getting home. "It's getting close to dinnertime," Alec said. "Don't you want to call your dad and tell him where you are or anything?"

"That's okay," Mora said quickly. "He doesn't get

back from the boat until later, and Aunt Sharon is at the pub."

"You should be getting home, just the same," Alec said. "Don't worry about your buddy here. I'll see to him. You can come back and check on him in the morning."

"You sure?" Mora said. "I could sleep out in the barn. I'm sure it would be okay with my dad."

Alec laughed. "I'll bet. Go home, would you please? Everything will be fine here."

"I'm going. I'm going," Mora said as she back-stepped up the aisle. Leaving the barn, she turned toward the lane but must have circled around and returned, because fifteen minutes later, when he looked out the kitchen window, Alec saw her run out of the barn a second time and start down the lane again.

9

BEACH THERAPY

ALEC CLIMBED OUT of bed before dawn the next morning. After a shower, a quick cup of tea and a piece of toast, he walked out to the barn. It was quiet and cozy-looking in the gray, early-morning light. When he reached the barn, he found Mora was already there, standing sentry outside the pony's stall. "You're up bright and early," Alec said.

"I couldn't sleep," Mora said.

Alec walked over to the feed bin and set to getting the Black's breakfast, and Mora tagged along behind him. "How long have you been here, anyway?" Alec asked.

"Oh, I, uh, just got here." Her eyes shifted away from his and he wondered if she was telling the truth. He wouldn't have been surprised if she'd been there for hours.

"Oh, I see. I just hope your dad knows that you are here. Maybe we should call him."

"It's okay with him," Mora said. "And he's gone already himself. He's always up early to get to the boat. Aunt Sharon is there, but she's still asleep."

Alec opened the Black's stall door and emptied the pail of oats into the feed trough. The stallion began eating hungrily. Alec stepped out of the stall again.

"So what's your story, Mora?" Alec asked. "With you and your family, I mean. You said you're from Ohio?"

"I was born here," Mora said, "and lived in Ireland when I was little, but I barely remember it. Then we moved to where my mom's from, in Ohio. My dad is a musician. He and his band were on tour a lot. Anyway, Mom and Dad divorced a couple years ago and Dad moved back to Ireland. This year they both decided I should spend the summer here."

"What's it like having a dad who is a musician?"

"Great. You get to meet all sorts of interesting people. Right now he's been spending more time fishing than playing music. Only the fishing isn't so good these days. Sometimes his boat stays out for days at a time."

"What do you do when he's away?"

"My aunt Sharon lives with us. She's nice. She's a musician too. She's a little older than my dad and works at the pub. Our house is on the other side of Oorloch. It's still only about five minutes away on my bike."

"Nothing seems too far away in this place," Alec said. "That's one thing I like about it."

"Are you taking the Black out today?" she asked. "What are you going to do?"

"More of the same," Alec said. "Go to the beach." Just then he heard the sound of a car motoring up the lane.

"That must be Bartley," Alec said. "I need to get going, but I'll wait until he gets here so I can introduce you. Bartley's okay. I think you two will get along."

Alec heard a car door slam. Bartley came straight to where they were standing and peered through the open half door. "So this is the mystery horse. Seems healthy enough. Can't say I've ever seen him before." He turned to face Mora. "You must be the lass who found him."

"This is Mora," Alec said. "She's new in town. From Ohio, the only state in the U.S. that is round on each end and high in the middle." Alec's weak attempt to get Mora to smile fell flat. Bartley didn't get it either.

"It's a joke," Alec said. "Round on the ends? High in the middle? O-hi-o. Get it?" Mora finally let a half-embarrassed smile redden her cheeks and brighten her face.

Bartley gave Alec a patient smile and then turned to Mora. "Well, then," he said, clapping his hands together softly. "I best be getting my horses their breakfast. I'll see to this one as well." He turned his head in the direction of the pony's stall. "Come along with me, young lady. You can take him out to the pasture after that."

"I'll be back soon," Alec said, then turned to Mora. "Have fun."

"I will," she said.

Alec nodded and walked over to the Black's side of the barn. He hoped it was all right leaving the pony with Mora. Bartley would be there but he'd be busy. They would be pretty much on their own.

A few minutes later, after breakfast and a light brushing for the Black, Alec threw a bottle of water and his book in a shoulder bag and slung it over his shoulder. Soon he was leading the Black out of the barn and down the lane to the beach.

The sky was clear, the wind cool and offshore. With the lower tide this morning came a wide expanse of wet, hard-packed sand stretching to the shoreline. They ambled along the water's edge, watching the birds dive, swoop and hover. Alec sang softly to the Black as they strolled along. The Black kept his ears pricked forward and neck arched high. Alec scanned the waves for seals but didn't see any.

They walked all the way to their favorite tide pool, where Alec led the Black in slow circles through the knee-deep water. Every so often they would stop and stand still, soak their feet, then start up again. Alec was glad he had remembered to bring his paperback mystery novel with him and read a few pages to pass the time as they walked along. It was getting to the good part of the book—the police were closing in on the ex–bank robber hero who was holed up in a mountain cabin after being forced to pull one last job for a corrupt politician.

The Black paced lazily around the tide pool as Alec let his attention shift between his book, the beach and the action of the Black's stride through the water. After a while they migrated to another tide pool adjacent to their regular spot. The water was shallower there, little more than ankle deep, and made for easier going. Soon Alec was alternating between pools, one lap in each, making for a perfect mixed-resistance workout for the Black.

Alec was curious to see what was happening with Mora and her pony back at the farm, so he decided to start home from their walk a little early. He wasn't wearing his watch, but his stomach told him that it must be around lunchtime. They crossed the beach, then wound their way through the dunes to the place where the path reached the lane. After another short walk up the sandy lane they turned off onto the driveway. In the distance Alec could see the pony in the far pasture. Mora was with him, sitting astride the pony's bare back.

"Oh boy," Alec said aloud, slapping his forehead. He should have known Mora would try something like that, should have known that she wouldn't be able to resist climbing up onto the pony, a horse she didn't know the first thing about. But Alec couldn't be too upset about it. He probably would have done the same thing if he were in her shoes.

"Hey," he called when he reached the pasture. Silver stood quiet and still as Mora dismounted.

Alec came closer. "Listen, Mora," he said. "I know you're anxious to ride, but you better be careful around here. We can take the pony down to the beach and you can ride him there if you want to. It might be safer and it would make me feel better to see how you handle yourself on a horse."

The Black, who had been standing with his eyes fixed firmly on the pony, pulled back on his lead suddenly, restless to get moving. "Let me put the Black away," Alec said. "We'll get something to eat. After that we can take the pony down to the beach and you can show me what you know."

"Sounds good to me," Mora said.

Back in the barn after lunch, Alec found a riding helmet, an old western saddle, pads and a bridle in the tack room. He carried them up the barn aisle to where Mora waited, holding the pony's head. Alec laid out the armful of gear on a bench.

Switching positions, Alec stood by the pony's head as Mora set to the job of saddling him up. First she centered the pad across the pony's spine. Then she picked up the heavy saddle and heaved it over the pad. The pony behaved himself beautifully, standing calm and still. Next, Mora hooked the left stirrup onto the pommel and set to buckling up the girth strap.

Alec watched as she gave the pony a couple gentle whacks in the stomach in case he was faking a bloat, trying to fool her into belting on the saddle more loosely than she intended. It was a common trick played by all sorts of riding horses, and Alec was glad to see Mora knew about it.

The pony sucked in his belly enough so Mora could buckle up the girth strap properly. She looped the remaining strap through a saddle ring, then knotted a flat knot and let the stirrup flap back down. Alec stepped in to check the tension in the girth, seeing how many fingers he could wriggle under the strap. The tension felt just about right.

"Good job," Alec said. "Now let's see how he takes to the bit." Mora picked up the worn but sturdy leather bridle and slipped it over the pony's head. Using a bit of sugar for encouragement, she nimbly slid the bit between the pony's teeth. "That's fine," Alec said. "Now let's get him down to the beach. We can mount up down there." Mora buckled up the chin strap on her riding helmet, eager to get going.

When they reached the beach Alec found a flat area between the dunes that made for a small three-sided canyon that would suit their needs. It was about fifty yards wide and as enclosed an area as they were likely to find here. Alec didn't want to chase Silver around any more than he had to if the pony decided to run off suddenly.

Alec waved Mora back and then swung up into the pony's saddle. "Watch me first," he said. He glanced at Mora and saw her expression change slightly and a flash of jealousy sparkle in her eyes.

Settling himself on the pony's back, Alec clucked once. With a light touch of his heels, he moved the pony into a brisk walk. The pony bobbled slightly as Alec pushed him into a trot. Alec stayed out of the way as the pony gathered himself. After a moment he let the pony know he was there again, keeping him to a regular gait, guiding him in a lazy figure-eight pattern. In motion, the pony's stride was smooth, even graceful. After a few stubborn stops and starts he was changing leads, even at a quick trot.

"He's a good boy," Alec said aloud, turning the pony back to where Mora was waiting. Alec pulled the pony to a stop. He backed him up six small steps, stopped again and hopped down. The pony tossed his head, and Alec gave him a pat on the neck.

Mora watched them, her eyes filled with more admiration than jealousy now. "You give him a try now," Alec said, taking the reins and holding them out to her. Mora made no move to take them.

"That was so . . . cool," she said. "You made it look so easy. He seemed to know exactly what you wanted him to do."

"You have to work hard to make it look easy," Alec said. "This boy doesn't seem to be a fighter, and he's definitely been schooled somewhere along the line. But there's always going to be resistance. It's the same with any horse." He pressed the reins into Mora's hands. "Now you try."

This time Mora took the reins, and a moment later Alec boosted her up into the saddle. She sat very straight, fiddling with the reins in her hands.

"Relax," Alec called. "Forget about your hands."

"Okay. Okay," Mora called back, her voice excited. She kept her eyes focused straight ahead.

"Relax," Alec called again. "Just ride around in a circle for now. And use your legs. Don't pull his head with the reins."

Mora took a deep breath and nudged the pony

into a walk. After a moment the serious expression on her face softened. "That's right," Alec said. "Bend him with your legs." She circled the alcove in the dunes a few times, first one way, then the other. "That's good," Alec said finally. "Now let's go down to the beach, where we'll have a little more room."

They crossed between the dunes and out onto the wide flats that stretched all the way to the water's edge. Alec led the way as Mora walked the pony to the water, then turned him around.

"Okay," Alec said. "Ride him back the way we just came. Try to keep him in a straight line and follow the tracks in the sand. You can trot him, but take it easy. Just ride to the edge of the dunes and then back. Go slow."

Mora did fine with the pony at first, riding straight and true, trotting off quickly, then slowing as they followed the track back to the dunes. It was after she turned the pony around and was on the way back that she got into trouble. She started off slow, and then, halfway to where Alec was standing, the pony began to speed up. Mora did nothing to stop him, and very quickly the speed made it difficult for her to keep her seat. She gave the reins a hurried tug, but it was too late. The pony stuck his nose out and accelerated, veering to one side, heading straight for the water at something close to a full gallop, as if he didn't have the slightest intention of stopping. His eyes came alive, flashing with fire.

There was no way Alec could head them off, but he did what he could, chasing after them and waving his arms. The pony flew across the flat sand and splashed into the water, Mora bouncing around wildly on his back. The pony charged through the shallows, then jerked to a stop as he reached the deeper water. Mora rocked forward on his neck, almost falling off.

The pony backed up a step, then stood still, staring out to sea. Finally Mora was able to get him turned around, out of the water and up on the beach again.

Alec walked out to them. "I saw that coming," he said. "You have to check him right away if he even hints at running off like that. You let it go too long and he took advantage. Check him right away next time. Not hard, just let him know you are there, lightly, at the right time."

"But . . . how do I know when that is?"

"You'll know."

"Easy for you to say."

"Just ride light," Alec said. "And listen to him. Listen with your hands and legs. Listen before you start talking. If you signal lightly he'll answer you the same way. If you saw on the reins or jerk at him, he'll jerk back. Now try it again. And pay attention this time."

Mora spoke to the pony and he trotted off toward the dunes again, one ear cocked back, a gleam in his eye. He was still full of himself, after his little run. Once again he tried to take charge, but this time Mora was able to steady him almost immediately. He tried again and Mora quickly checked him again. Finally he seemed to accept the fact that Mora was in charge, for the time being anyway.

So it went for another hour, Mora trying to stay focused, Alec reminding her to stay light and use her legs, the pony trying to take advantage if Mora relaxed a little too much. Finally Alec held up his hand. "That's enough for today, I think. He's getting hot."

Mora slid out of the saddle. Alec slipped her a piece of carrot and she gave it to the very grateful pony. "This is the time for treats," Alec said. "Come on. Let's get back to the barn."

As they walked along Mora turned to Alec. "I was trying to listen, like you said, and anticipate his next move. I thought I was getting it, but I'm not really sure. He might just be tired."

Alec nodded. "He's getting tired, but you were doing better at the end there. Just keep your mind on your riding. This pony isn't the kind of horse you can get too relaxed on. He may be well trained, but that only counts for so much. It's the same with any horse. If you don't look where you're going, you'll wind up where you're not looking."

"You mean I always have to keep up my guard with him?"

"No, of course not. You just need to know when you can relax and when you can't. You'll learn."

They walked back to the barn, the pony following obediently beside Mora. It was hard to know what to make of this guy, Alec thought, all fired up one moment, docile and well mannered the next. What had Silver been thinking, trying to run off into the water at a full gallop like that? Alec wondered. He hadn't been panicking. The look in his eyes had been anything but fear, more like fierce determination, the look of a come-from-behind racehorse bearing down on the finish line. It was so intense it was almost scary.

10

the storm

ThAT NIGhT, AFTER he'd eaten and washed up his dinner dishes, Alec picked up the phone and called the police station. The officer he spoke with was understanding, and tried to be helpful, but said there was absolutely nothing more he could do. He had contacted all the local stables, and all their horses were accounted for. He asked Alec if he would like the phone number for the county animal control department. Alec said that wouldn't be necessary. The officer suggested Alec put a notice in the lost-and-found section of the local newspaper. Alec thanked him and said he'd do just that if no one claimed the pony by tomorrow.

The next morning Alec was up early, as usual. He ate a quick bowl of cereal and then stepped outside. Filling his lungs with the cool, clean sea air, he strolled over to the barn. Mora was there, waiting on a bench outside the barn door. She dug in a pocket of her jeans and held out a few crumpled bills. "I brought some money this morning too, to pay for Silver's feed . . . and everything."

Alec pushed her hand away. "You can talk to Tom about that when he gets here," he said. "Let's get these horses fed, then we'll hit the beach." Alec slid open the heavy barn door. "I mean," he called back over his shoulder, "if you're up for it."

"Am I!" Mora said, rushing past Alec to Silver's stall.

They started off down the lane and into the dunes, following the trail to the beach. Mora rode on ahead while Alec walked beside the Black, holding the lead line loosely in his hand. The stallion's gait was smooth and regular. He seemed to have recovered completely from his pulled muscle and had stopped limping days ago. The Black usually healed well, but Alec wasn't discounting the medicinal benefits of their therapy sessions in the tide pools.

They rounded the first bend in the coastline and passed the place where he and Mora first met. They continued on and Alec noticed how wide the beach was this morning. The tide must be farther out than on previous mornings, he guessed. He wondered if there would even be any water in their favorite Jacuzzi pool for the day's therapy session.

When they arrived at the pool he was glad to see it was still filled with water, though the Jacuzzi effect, the in-and-out rush of water from the waves, was not happening. Alec slipped out of his sneakers and led the Black into the tide pool. The water was surprisingly warm. For the moment the Black was content to stand still and enjoy it, steady on all four feet. Alec found a seat, drinking in the wild loneliness of the sea-ravaged coastline. He leaned back against a rock, pulled his paperback from his jacket pocket and started to read.

After an hour or so he looked up from his book to catch sight of Mora riding her pony in wide loopy circles down where the dunes ended and the cliffs began. She was a fairly decent rider, Alec thought, with a natural sense of balance. Maybe a little too fearless for her own good, not that he was anyone to judge on that score. He'd done plenty of crazy things on horseback himself, more than once surviving due to blind luck rather than any great skill on his part.

The Black was beginning to act restless suddenly, pawing the water, snorting and flaring his nostrils. Alec followed the stallion's gaze and saw he was watching Mora gallop the pony along the shoreline.

"Okay, okay," Alec said to his horse finally. "You're getting bored. I get the message. Let's take a walk."

Alec kept the Black on his lead line as they made their way along the water's edge to the far side of the beach. Silver and Mora were capering ahead, following the shoreline all the way to the cliffs, then out to the point. He certainly was light-footed for a chunky little pony, Alec thought.

When Alec and the Black finally reached them, Mora had dismounted and was standing beside Silver.

"You two seem to be getting on well today," Alec said.

"Thanks," Mora said. "That lesson you gave me yesterday helped a lot." She gave the pony a warm pat on the neck. "Of course it helps to be partnered with a pony like Silver. He's a good boy, yes, he is."

Again Alec had to laugh at himself when he remembered his first impression of this pony, the time he'd glimpsed him among the rocks at the point the other day. How had he ever mistaken this gentle pony for an angry stallion? Alec asked himself. This fellow seemed about as friendly a horse as old Napoleon, the Black's faithful stable pony back home at Hopeful Farm. And yet the Black still seemed a bit wary of Silver for some reason. That wasn't too surprising, Alec thought. The stallion was always cautious around other horses, always ready to run, or fight, especially with the males, even geldings. This time it seemed the Black sensed something else. At least they weren't fighting.

The weather this morning was clear and sunny with not a cloud in the sky. The offshore breeze that had been blowing all morning had dwindled down until now there was hardly any wind at all.

"Pretty nice with the tide so far out," Mora said. "You could ride the beach for miles today if you wanted to."

Something splashed in the water out by the rocks just offshore. "Hey, look," Alec said. "It's a seal."

Mora turned to where Alec was pointing. Just then Silver, who'd been standing peacefully beside Mora and behaving himself all this time, suddenly decided to get frisky. With a quick snap of his head, he jerked back on his reins. Mora was caught by surprise and the reins slipped from her grip.

"Come back here," she cried as the pony trotted off. Silver ignored her, zigzagging out among the rocks with his tail held high. In a moment he disappeared from view. Mora chased after him and soon vanished around the point as well.

Alec called to Mora but heard no answer back. After a minute he decided he'd better see what had happened to her. Following the tracks in the sand, Alec led the Black past wave-weathered rocks and continued along a pathway of wet sand left by the receding tide.

The cliffs here were cut from layers of colored rock different from those on the other side of the point, perhaps limestone and slate, lighter rock layered between darker. Somehow, to Alec, it brought to mind a gigantic layered cake, though there was also something dark and ominous about the high, cathedral-like walls.

The path threaded its way between the rocks and forbidding cliff face. Jagged escarpments, like balconies of stone, loomed above. Wind- and wave-carved rocks rose up from the sand on either side like unfinished statues. Soon they passed through a cavernous doorway between the rocks that became a short tunnel beneath a low overhanging ledge. Tangled knots of driftwood and heavy, gnarled logs lay strewn about, half buried in the sand, probably washed in from some nearby river after a storm.

Rounding the edge of the point, Alec followed the path until it opened up into a half-moon-shaped cove. A wide, white sand beach spread out before him, bordered by sheer cliffs hundreds of feet high on one side and the sea on the other. Another rock point bookended the cove at the opposite end.

Mora was down by the water, not fifty yards away, but there was no sign of Silver.

"Did you see him?" Alec asked. "Where did he go?"

Mora shrugged her shoulders. "I found some tracks here," she said, pointing to a trail of hoofprints down by the water's edge. "Let's see were they lead."

They walked for a minute, but Silver seemed to

have vanished completely. Even his tracks were washing away in the waves. Alec watched the Black for some sign to tell them where to look, but the stallion's actions told him nothing. Surely if Silver was nearby the Black should scent him, yet from all Alec could tell the Black was as puzzled as Alec and Mora.

"Hey, Alec," Mora said. "Is that a person? How in the world did he get up there?"

"Where?"

"On that rock." Alec turned toward the water to look where she was pointing, the top of a single enormous rock, rising up like a monolith out of the sea about fifty feet from shore. The rock island looked to be close to one hundred feet high with sheer edges on either side, perhaps all that was left of a ridge broken off into the sea centuries ago.

At first Alec thought he saw what Mora was talking about, a dark shape that might have been a person standing on a stone balcony at the very top of the rock. But then, when he looked again, whatever it was seemed to have vanished.

"I don't see anything."

"There," Mora said, pointing to the jutting promontory where dark-winged seabirds clung to the nooks in the rock face.

"That's a bird."

"No, it was . . . just there," Mora said, then

rubbed her hand over her face. "But you are right. I don't see anything there now."

"Must have been a bird," Alec said again. "Anyhow, it doesn't look to me like there's any way for a person to get up there. Not unless he could fly. Come on, let's go."

Alec gazed up at the looming cliffs as they walked along. Somehow this place brought to mind some great stadium or amphitheater, he thought, a place where the sea performed a never-ending show for the birds watching from their seats in the cliff face above.

Mora pointed out the shadowy mouth of a cave at the base of the cliff. It was wide enough to accommodate a horse and she wondered if Silver might not have found his way into it. Alec didn't think so. "There would be tracks in the sand leading there if that was the case," he said.

They came to a place where a cluster of column-shaped rocks rose up from the sand. Alec was admiring the weird, otherworldly shapes of the towers when the Black suddenly gave a shrill neigh and lunged against his lead line. Alec managed to hold him still and turned to look where the Black was now staring. Not more than a hundred yards behind them, Alec saw Silver ambling across the sand.

Alec couldn't believe it. How did the pony get behind them?

"He must have doubled back somehow," Mora said. "Maybe he was in that cave all along."

Silver seemed fine, but immediately Alec noticed that the pony was bareback now. Mora caught hold of Silver's bridle and scolded him for running off. The pony lowered his head and nudged her shoulder.

"Where's Tom's saddle?" Alec asked.

"Maybe he rubbed up against the rocks and slipped it off somehow," Mora said.

"The girth strap was that loose?" Alec asked.

Mora shook her head. "I thought I cinched him up tight. You checked it yourself, didn't you?" Alec had to admit that the strap had seemed secure when they left the barn.

"It must have come loose during the ride somehow. You were riding him before. Are you sure you didn't notice anything off?"

Mora shook her head. "It wasn't slipping. I don't know what happened."

A cool gust of wind swept in from the sea suddenly and Alec could see the edge of dark clouds moving closer beyond the farthest point. "Looks like some weather is coming," he said. "We better get going."

After a short search they found the missing saddle among some rocks. Alec leaned down to pick it up from the sand and noticed the leather was not even scuffed. He checked the girth strap. It was old but certainly not worn out. How had it come undone? he wondered. And if the pony rubbed up against the rocks to get his saddle off, why wasn't it scraped up? It just didn't make sense.

Alec cleaned off the saddle, wiping away the splotches of sand.

"Could he have rolled on the ground and gotten the saddle loose that way?" Mora asked. Alec looked at Silver, who stood still, watching them. His coat was flecked with bits of sand, but not enough to make it look as if he had been rolling on the ground.

"I don't think so," Alec said. "He'd be covered in sand if he'd done that."

"Maybe not," Mora said. "The sand close to the water seems as hard as pavement."

"I suppose," Alec said. He stepped over beside the pony and ran his hand down Silver's neck. "But you'd think his coat would still get wet. He feels almost dry to me."

Mora shrugged. "I can't think of any other way it could've happened."

Mora held Silver's head while Alec gently placed the saddle on the pony's back and cinched up the girth strap. Again he noticed that it seemed to be in perfect shape. Maybe the strap wasn't the problem at all.

The pony gave a little grunt but otherwise stood by calmly as Alec cinched up the strap an extra hole to make sure it didn't slip off again. "That should hold you," Alec said.

The wind was blowing stronger and the sky became darker. The surface of the sea, placid all morning, was now shattered with whitecaps. All at once a booming sound cracked overhead. It was loud enough that at first Alec thought part of the cliff must have given way in a rock slide. He instinctively threw himself up against the Black, pushing the stallion away from the cliff and out to the water's edge. Mora quickly pulled the gray pony over to the water as well.

"What was that?" Mora said. "It sounded like an explosion."

Alec looked up, glad to see nothing falling down on top of him from above. "You okay?" he asked Mora.

"I'm all right," she said.

"Let's get out of here before we get totally soaked." A moment later there was another boom, this one accompanied by a flash of lightning in the sky. A rush of rain and wind swept down upon them. Alec could see whitecaps roiling the water into a violent chop offshore. From somewhere the bark of a dog flew by. Or, Alec thought, was it the bark of a seal?

With a tight hold on the halters, Alec and Mora led the Black and Silver back the way they'd come, quickly finding shelter among the rocks in the tunnel-like passageway beneath the cliffs. They huddled together as the torrent of wind and rain whipped by outside. Thankfully it was more or less dry inside the tunnel and a good place to hole up and wait out the storm.

After a few minutes the storm passed with the same sudden rush with which it had arrived. The wind slackened and the rain let up. As the rain softened to a drizzle, they started off again, making their way through the rocks to the other side of the point and along the beach toward the farm. Once, when Alec turned to look back toward the far point, he thought he saw something in the water just offshore, a dark shadow moving in the face of a breaking wave. He watched a moment and then saw a seal raise its head above the surface. Treading water, the seal turned toward the beach, as if it was watching them.

"There's that seal again," he said. As Mora turned, the seal rolled onto its back, swam in a sleek circle, then dipped below the surface and was gone.

11

THE GIRL
IN THE DUNES

THE SUN WAS well out again when Alec and Mora reached the farm. There were few puddles and it seemed as if it had barely rained at all there. Alec ran up to the house and found some towels so they could dry off a little. He and Mora gave their horses quick baths, sponging them off with warm water and then walking them in the glistening sunshine to dry.

After the horses were turned out into the pasture, Alec walked back to the barn, where he found Bartley in the aisle brushing out one of the Irish hunters. When he commented on the sudden cloud burst, Bartley nodded and smiled. "You'll have that this time of year," Bartley said. "Local squalls will blow up out of nowhere, especially along the coast here. You get used to it."

Mora was determined to hang around, so the stable manager put her to work mucking out stalls. Alec

121

told Bartley about the saddle slipping and they looked it over together. Neither of them could find anything out of order, but Bartley suggested using another saddle the next time Mora went riding. Luckily Tom kept plenty of extra saddles and tack around for the folks who rented his horses.

After dinner that evening, Alec checked the phone messages one more time. There were still no calls from anyone looking for a missing pony. Alec thought of calling the police station again but then decided against it. Surely they would have notified him if they had any news.

And then a thought crossed his mind suddenly. What if no one showed up to claim the pony? What if Silver had simply been abandoned? Alec hadn't really considered that possibility. He'd always assumed that a saddle-wise pony like Silver, or whatever his real name was, must belong to somebody. But now he wasn't so sure what to think.

Alec shook his head. What have I gotten Tom into? he thought. But there was no point in worrying about it. Better to do something . . . like call the newspaper and place that notice in the lost-and-found column. He picked up a pen and paper and set to composing his notice. He didn't want to get too specific. If more than one person showed up to claim the pony, details that only the owner could know might help identify the true owner. After a minute he came up with this:

> Found—Saddle Pony on Oorloch Strand—Seeking
> information regarding identity of pony found
> wandering on the beach near Oorloch last
> Sunday. Saddle-wise pony of mixed breed, gray
> with pale mane and tail, appears to have been
> living in the open for several days. If you lost
> a pony, or know who he might belong to,
> please contact the Dailey Farm in Oorloch.

Alec called the local newspaper, and a man took down his information and told Alec the notice would run in the day after tomorrow's edition and for the week after that. Next he made a phone call to Tom Dailey. Tom's colt was racing tomorrow afternoon and Tom sounded excited. When Alec reported that no one had called about collecting the lost pony yet, Tom said not to worry. Maybe the pony showing up when he did was a good sign. Maybe he would bring them luck in the race.

Henry got on the line. He said Tom was acting as nervous as a bridegroom about this race. Henry asked about the Black and Alec told him that the stallion seemed fine, fit enough to ride, and that he was think-ing of doing just that tomorrow morning.

"He's your horse," Henry said. "You know him better than anyone else. If you think he's fit enough to ride, ride him. The sooner the better, I'd say."

The next morning, Alec drank a quick cup of tea and then walked down to the barn. Mora had prom-ised to be there early and he half expected to see her waiting there. She wasn't. Alec fed the Black and gave Silver his morning oats as well.

The horses finished their breakfast, and, when Mora still didn't show up, Alec figured he might as well give the pony a quick grooming. Taking the hal-ter off the hook, Alec unlatched the stall door and stepped inside.

"Hey, boy," he called. The pony returned Alec's greeting with a soft nicker. Alec slipped the halter over the pony's head and buckled it on. Silver began nudg-ing Alec's pockets.

"You're no dummy," Alec said. "You know who the treat meister is around here." He fished in his pocket and pulled out a carrot stick. Breaking it in half, he fed it to the pony, one piece at a time.

After a minute Alec led the pony out of his stall and tied him in the aisle. He was just about to get started when he heard the sound of someone running up the aisle. It was Mora. "Sorry I'm late," she said. "My bike had a flat tire."

"Well, you're here now," Alec said, "so why don't you take over here?"

Alec handed Mora the brush and she set to work. Alec was glad to see the ease with which she set about the job. The pony stood still as Mora worked. He certainly seemed accustomed to being handled, though he had his sensitive spots, just like any horse. Mora flinched when she hit one ticklish spot on his hindquarters and the pony jerked his hind hoof.

"Don't do that," Alec said. "Don't ever seem to be afraid of him. He's not a kicker, and if he were one, stepping back would be the worst thing to do. Stay close to a kicker. That way he can't get much behind it in case he decides to take a swing."

They heard the sound of Bartley's car rattling up the driveway and a moment later Bartley came through the door. After exchanging hellos, Mora asked if there was anything she could do around the barn. Bartley put her to work mucking out stalls and cleaning tack. The stable manager seemed pleased to have the unexpected help and Mora set upon her chores willingly, gladly offering her services in trade for the pony's room and board.

Soon Alec and the Black were down to the beach,

walking along the hard, wet sand by the water's edge. This was the day, Alec had decided. It was time to start riding the Black again.

Alec stopped the Black and waited until the stallion was completely calm. Then, leaning his chest and arms across the Black's sleek back, he eased on his weight until his tiptoes left the ground. Alec repeated this a few more times, letting the stallion hold his weight only for a moment or two at first, longer and longer each time after that. The Black remained calm and steady all the while. Finally Alec swung his leg up and was astride the Black for the first time since the race.

The stallion moved easily along the beach, the rhythm of his movements strong and regular. After a minute Alec slid off the stallion's back. Leaning down, he ran his hands over the Black's left rear leg, feeling for any extra heat in the tendon and finding none. The Black snorted impatiently as Alec handled his legs. Then Alec slowly, carefully hoisted himself up onto the stallion's back again. He rode on some more, and then walked again. Alec could still feel nothing unusual or out of step in the Black's overstriding gait, at least nothing obvious.

"That's a boy," he said softly. "Let's take it easy now."

The Black looked back at Alec, staring straight into his eyes with a long, mesmerizing gaze. Again Alec

spoke to his horse and the Black turned his head sideways and back and forth as if to signal his understanding.

They rode a short way down the beach and came
to their favorite tide pool. Taking up a seat on a flat
rock, Alec pulled out his paperback and started to read
while the Black cooled his heels in the water.

As the sun rose higher, the weather became almost
hot. Soon Alec found himself thinking about lunch. He
had noticed he was feeling hungrier than usual here.
Perhaps it was the brisk sea air, or maybe it was just
Mrs. Pierce's cooking. They started back to the farm.

Alec had become so accustomed to being alone
with the Black here that he was surprised to notice
someone fishing up the beach. As Alec came closer he
saw it was an older man about his dad's age, wearing
a floppy hat.

The man waved Alec over. Alec nodded hello as
the Black eyed the fishing rod in the man's hand
warily.

"Good day to you, lad," the fisherman said,
touching the brim of his hat in a friendly salute. He
was a small, rabbit-faced man with freckles, dressed
in a long, sun-faded topcoat, like something a sea cap-
tain from another era might wear. The Black danced in
place and pulled back.

"Easy, boy," Alec said, moving with his horse.

"I'd appreciate it if you could take it easy with that fishing rod," Alec called to the man. "My horse has an aversion to anything that looks even remotely like a lash whip."

The man lowered his fishing rod. "Sorry," he said. "I didn't mean to startle him. You must be the Yank with the racehorse that's staying at Dailey's farm."

"Alec Ramsay," Alec said.

"Mike Malloy," the fisherman said. "Good to meet you. And good to see someone appreciate the beach around here. The locals seem to have forgotten all about it these days."

"It's a treat for us. The Black loves the beach. We've been walking it every day, morning and afternoon."

"Nowhere better than here, lad."

"Ever been to that cove around the far point?" Alec asked. "How's the fishing over there?"

Mike shook his head slightly. "Never go over there. No one does. Fishing's no good on that side." The man gave Alec a wry smile. "These days it's not so hot here either, one reason why you don't see too many folks out on the beach."

"I was wondering about that," Alec said.

"I still like to come down here myself," Mike said, "especially since the wife passed. Still like to throw the line in the water, practice my casting and watch for birds and seals. They'll generally tell you where the fish are."

"I saw a seal yesterday. I almost thought he was following me."

"A seal?" the fisherman said. "I haven't seen any in a while myself. Few fish either, for that matter. Mostly I'm just looking for pieces of driftwood. I whittle 'em down at night, you see. After a week or so I work them into something like . . . Here, let me show you." The man reached into his coat pocket and pulled out a small wooden object, a carved figurine shaped like a woman with the tail of a fish.

"Nice," Alec said.

"I sell them to tourists over the holidays. This one is my little mermaid," he said. He searched around a canvas bag slung over his shoulder and pulled out a few other small chunks of wood. "I'm going to carve these into chess pieces for a chess set. I use polished stones for the pawns," he explained, "wood for the rest. When I'm done, they look like this." He dug into his bag again and produced three small wooden figures that he forced into Alec's hand. "The king is a bull, the queen a stag. The knights are horses, of course."

"Of course," Alec said, not really sure what the old guy was talking about. He turned the carved chess pieces over in his hand and admired the fine workmanship.

"Very nice," Alec said politely, then handed them back. The Black tossed his head impatiently, still not liking the looks of Mike's fishing rod. Alec said they'd better be going.

"Pleasure to meet you," the man called over his shoulder as Alec led the Black up the beach.

"Likewise," Alec called back. "Hope to see you again."

Alec and the Black walked farther along the empty beach, and as they neared the turnoff to the road Alec saw someone standing up in the high dunes. It was Mora—at least that was what Alec thought at the time. At first she didn't seem to notice him. It looked as if she was doing yoga exercises or something, spinning her arms, rolling her neck and twisting her waist. Then she stopped suddenly, turned to face him and began to wave.

Alec waved back and walked closer, wondering what she wanted. All at once the Black flung his head and froze in step. The stallion stared off to the dunes and sniffed the air, his body tense, as if sensing danger there. Alec moved closer to the Black's head and took up the slack in the lead line. "Easy, boy," he said. "It's just Mora."

The girl continued to beckon and then stepped behind a high dune to disappear from view. Alec led the uneasy stallion around to the other side of the dune and looked to the spot where the girl had been standing. She wasn't there.

Alec looked over to where the road led back to the farm and didn't see her on the road either. Where was she? he wondered. She couldn't have run ahead to the farm that fast, Alec thought. Maybe she was riding her bike.

Odd that she seemed to be calling to him but wouldn't wait to tell him what she wanted. And what was she doing there in the first place? Alec felt a little uncomfortable about it all and hurried back to the farm. When he arrived, he saw Mora walking Silver down from the far pasture.

"What's going on?" Alec asked when he reached them. "I thought the pony was penned up."

"He escaped," she said. "I went in the barn for a minute, came back and he was gone. The paddock gate was open. At first I thought you'd taken him out for some reason. But then I thought about it some more and figured you would never have left the gate open. Anyway, I looked all over and found him outside the fence up on top of the hill."

"You mean you were here at the farm the whole time?" Alec asked.

"Sure," Mora said. "Where'd you think I'd be?"

"You weren't down on the beach just now, up in the dunes? I saw a girl there. I thought it was you. I waved and whoever it was waved back. I could have sworn it was you."

She shook her head. "Not me," she said with a smile. "Maybe you have a secret admirer."

"How'd Silver get out the gate?" Alec asked.

"I have no idea," she said. "I thought it was closed. The latch must have slipped."

"I'll look at it," Alec said, "though it didn't seem loose to me before or I would have noticed. Some horses can slip a latch by nibbling at it. But I don't see how the pony could have even reached this one unless he stood up on his hind legs. It's set up too high."

Alec turned the Black loose in his pasture. He checked the gate latch in Silver's paddock. It seemed to be working perfectly. He walked back to the house, went inside and checked the messages on the answering machine. There was no news from Tom. No one had called regarding Silver either. Well, he thought, the notice was coming out in the newspaper the next morning. If no one showed up to claim the pony after that, then he'd just have to assume someone simply abandoned him.

Later that afternoon, Alec joined Mora as she led Silver out to the pasture. The pony played with the lead line in Mora's hands. His neck rose in a proud curve that ran all the way up to his ears. She reached up and rubbed his forehead.

"What do you think, Alec?" she said. "Isn't he a good boy?"

"When he's not picking locks," Alec said.

"I wish I could just keep him," Mora said.

"If no one claims him, maybe you can," Alec said, "if you are able to find a place where he can stay."

"Any chance that place might be here?" Mora asked cautiously.

"That would be up to Tom, not me," Alec said. "Anyhow, the chances are good that the owner is still out there looking for our wayward friend. You better give it a few more days before you start making too many plans."

"Where is Tom, anyway?" she asked. "Still at the track in England?" .

"His colt is running today," Alec said. "I guess we'll hear how he makes out soon enough."

But Tom didn't call that afternoon, or that evening either. Later that night, with still no word from Tom, Alec thought about calling down to the track. He picked up the phone and was about to dial Tom's number, but then changed his mind. Better to wait and see, Alec decided. Surely Tom would be in touch before long.

A FRIENDLY RACE

THE NEXT DAY a rain shower in the morning kept Alec and the Black in the barn later than usual. After the rain stopped, Alec and Mora rode their horses down to the beach. Again the Black seemed in fine shape. It was great to be riding again, Alec thought, and nice to have the company as well.

The two beach riders jogged their horses along the water's edge and didn't pull up until they reached the far point. They even thought about going around the point, but the tide was higher this morning and the path impassable. Mora pointed out footprints in the sand leading around the rocks and disappearing into the water.

"Looks like someone was out here this morning, though," Mora said. "Maybe it was that guy I saw up on the rock the other day. Maybe he was fishing or something."

"Sure," Alec said. "Maybe it was your birdman."

Mora smiled. "Or maybe it was your secret admirer from the dunes."

"Must be her," Alec said, playing along. "Your birdman would have flown up there. He wouldn't need to walk."

"Think what you want," she said. "I'm positive that was a person I saw on top of that rock the other day."

"I met a fisherman on the beach yesterday who told me that no one goes over to that side of the point. He said the fishing isn't very good over there. Then again, he said it isn't very good on this side either these days. Maybe he decided to give it a try over there this morning."

They turned around and Mora put the pony into a trot, then a gallop, chasing some birds skimming along the beach. Alec gave them a few lengths' head start and then took off after them, the stallion breaking into a run for the first time in a week.

The reins came alive in Alec's strong hands, seeming to vibrate in his palms. With a deep breath, Alec melded himself into the Black's bare back, pressing the side of his face flat against his horse's neck.

Soon they were completely in sync. What a joy to be running like this again, he thought. To Alec, when he was in flight with his horse, there seemed to be whole seconds between each stride, plenty of time to do whatever he needed to do. It was as if time itself were slowing down.

The stallion swallowed up the space between the pony and himself. His strides were lengthening, hanging longer, with more hesitation between each one. But then, as the Black pulled alongside Mora and the pony, something unexpected happened. Rather than blowing right by them, Silver began to pick up speed, refusing to be overtaken.

Tracking along beside the Black, the pony was taking three springy steps for every two of the Black's, matching the stallion's pace but on a shorter stride. Mora leaned forward as she tried to hang on. A look of panic flashed across the girl's face as she struggled to keep her seat.

The stallion asked for more speed but Alec held him back. This was way too fast, he thought, and way too soon. The Black hadn't run like this since his injury. It was crazy for him to feel so challenged by a pony like Silver, yet that was exactly what was happening. The Black fought for his head. Neither he nor the pony would give in, each pushing the other harder and harder.

"Hey," Alec called to Mora. "Slow down!"

"I'm trying!" she called back. Alec could see she was shifting her weight back and pulling on her reins, but Silver was not responding.

Suddenly Alec realized that not only was the pony running faster than Alec would ever have believed, but the girl had found her seat and was riding better too. At least she wasn't panicking or bouncing around now.

Alec returned all of his attention to his own horse, which was running like a freight train with the brakes on. He hauled the reins closer to his chest. Finally the Black responded and the pony began inching ahead, first by a nod, a nose, then a head and neck. When he was a length ahead, Silver eased off at last. Finally the two horses were slowing together.

"Woo-hoo," Mora hooted with delight.

Alec pulled up beside her. "Where did that come from?" he asked.

"I don't know," Mora said, catching her breath, "but it felt great."

"It didn't look like you were feeling so great for a while there," Alec said.

"I never expected it, that's for sure," she said. "Boy, he can run when he wants, can't he?"

The horses relaxed their jog to a walk. Alec shook his head. "I never would have believed it."

Mora gave the pony a pat on the neck. "After he got going he was running so smooth. It felt like we were flying. I don't know why. It just felt . . . perfect."

Alec wasn't sure what to say. In a way, he felt he should probably scold Mora for letting the pony get away from her like that. But she had handled herself capably and he couldn't be too mad at her about that.

"You did a good job of hanging on," he said finally. "I mean, it was crazy for you to go that fast, but you hung on and didn't fall off. That's the most important thing."

Mora bounced along in her saddle, smiling broadly and talking to her horse. Alec looked at Silver, who was tossing his head as if ready to go another half mile. How could this wiggling, waddling pony be the same horse that just tried to outrun the Black? It seemed impossible, but there it was.

"That was so cool," Mora said. "Want to race back to the farm?"

Alec shook his head. "No way," he said. "You wore us out. One gallop will be plenty for today, thank you. The Black is supposed to be on vacation, remember?"

Back at the farm, Alec turned the Black loose in his pasture, then came down to the barn. Bartley was at his desk looking over some paperwork. Alec stepped into the little alcove next to the tack room that served as the barn office and asked, "Have you heard from Tom yet?"

Bartley looked up from his work and shook his head. "No, he still hasn't called."

"That's odd," Alec said. "I wonder how the colt did in his race."

"He came in third," Bartley said. "I bought the paper this morning and they covered the race." He handed Alec the sports section of the newspaper. "Here, see for yourself."

Alec found the listing for the Collingswood race results and saw that Tom's colt was reported to have "finished driving" in his race.

"At least he placed in the money," Alec said. "It's certainly nothing to be ashamed of."

"You know how high Tom is on that colt," Bartley said. "He probably sulked a bit when Calypso didn't win. Anyhow, I guess we'll be hearing from him when he's ready to talk."

Turning from the sports to the classified section of the paper, Alec checked for his notice about the lost pony. It was there, all right, prominently placed at the top of the lost-and-found column.

Now we'll see if anyone turns up to claim the pony, Alec thought.

When he glanced through the rest of the pages, something in the local section caught his eye. It was an advertisement for an upcoming fair. Below an illustration of a Celtic harp, along with a horse, a sheep and a cow, was a headline that read "OLD FAIR DAY—Don't Miss the End of Summer Fleadh This Weekend!!!"

Alec pointed out the ad to Bartley. "Flea-dha?" he asked. "What's that?"

"It's an old-time music festival," Bartley said. "An end-of-summer tradition around here. You pronounce it Flah, by the way."

"Irish music?" Alec said. "Like bagpipes?"

"Aye, me boy," he said, putting on a thick Irish brogue. "Nothing else like it anywhere. You'll hear fiddles and flutes, golden harps and goatskin drums, guitars, banjos and accordions. 'Tis music for dancing, for love, for helping the ale slip down. Fine craic."

"Craic?" Alec asked.

Bartley gave Alec a sly wink and smiled. "It's a Gaelic word that can mean a lot of different things," he said. "For the most part it just means good times."

The phone on the desk began to ring and Bartley picked it up. "Hallo, Tom," he said, giving Alec an exaggerated wink. "Speak of the devil. We were figuring you'd be calling soon. . . . You don't say? . . . All of that, was he?"

After a minute, Bartley passed the phone over to Alec. Henry was on the line now. "So how did it go?" Alec asked.

"Oh, the colt did pretty well," Henry said. "Finished strong. He ran into some traffic at the start. But listen, that's not what I wanted to talk about. I just had a call from the airline. They said there is a shortage of stall space right now on the flights back to New York. It looks like you and the Black will be staying here a few extra days."

"What about you?"

"I made a reservation to go back this evening."

The news caught Alec by surprise. "Tonight?"

"Tonight," Henry said. "We've been away awhile and I don't want things to get too balled up back at the farm." Alec said that if that was what Henry wanted to do, it was fine with him.

When Tom came back on the line he reported that he would be taking the colt to visit a friend's farm to check out some of the local stock while he was in England and apologized because he wouldn't be returning to Oorloch for a few more days. Alec replied that there was no need for an apology, that all was well with the Black and that Bartley and Mrs. Pierce were taking good care of them. "We'll guard the fort until you get back," Alec said, and hung up the phone.

13

COFFEE WITH MRS. P.

NO ONE CALLED about the lost pony that evening, or the next day either. Alec spent his time down at the beach with the Black, sometimes with Mora and Silver, sometimes by themselves. The afternoons were getting hotter than ever. As Alec came into the kitchen to get a drink of water, he ran into Mrs. Pierce. The scent of spicy cardamom and coffee hung in the air.

"Hallo, lad," she said when she saw him. "Sit down. Have a drop of coffee." Her voice twanged, like a slightly out-of-tune Irish harp.

"Maybe I will," Alec said. "Just a small one." He pulled out a chair from the kitchen table and sat down. Mrs. Pierce put a ceramic cup down on the table in front of him and then retrieved a long-handled, brass-colored container from the stove.

Leaning over the table, Mrs. Pierce poured the thick black liquid into Alec's cup. Alec smiled. It was the sort of drink one might expect in Arabia, he thought, and seemed a little out of place here in this Irish kitchen.

"I thought everyone drank tea in Ireland," Alec said.

"Not everyone," she said. "My family has always enjoyed coffee in the afternoon. Especially good Turkish coffee like this. They stock it for me special down at Makem's store in town."

"It's always nice to have some variety," Alec said.

Mrs. Pierce smiled her gold-toothed smile. "Enjoy," she said.

She gave Alec a wink. She had a wrinkled, round face and a small bump of a nose. Her blue eyes were flecked with gray. Alec imagined that she must have been beautiful once.

They drank their coffee and talked about this and that, the weather and how Alec liked Ireland so far. Then Alec asked Mrs. Pierce to tell him more about herself and what it was like growing up with the Travelers in Ireland.

She took a sip of coffee and leaned back in her chair. "It was a hard life," she said, "but a good one. We never went hungry, but we certainly weren't rich. There was a time, when I was a little girl, my mother and I used to go peddling door-to-door."

"What did you sell?"

"Oh, anything small, paper flowers and little

carved wooden statues, feather fishing lures, reed baskets. Sometimes Mother would give psychic readings, read palms and tell fortunes and such. She taught me a thing or two about the art as well."

"Really?" Alec asked. "You can read fortunes?"

"Sometimes," she said. "Let me show you." She reached across the table and picked up Alec's coffee cup. "One way you can do it is like this." She took hold of Alec's wrist, pulling his hand toward her. "Take your thumb and rub it through the grinds at the bottom of your cup."

Alec pressed his thumb into the coffee grinds left in his cup as she'd asked. "That's right," she said. "What I'm looking for is an impression of your thumbprint. That's right, just smear it in there. It doesn't need to be clear."

Mrs. Pierce took the cup from him. She bent her head over the cup to study the contents. "Sometimes you can see things here, signs that tell what has come before, and what is to come." She glanced up at Alec, met his eyes and then looked back down again. She tilted the cup back and forth, rotated it in her hand. Without taking her eyes away from the cup in her hand, she began to speak, her voice soft and low.

"I can see you carry a weight on your heart. You have seen hard times. Perhaps lost someone you loved? I see you walking down a country road, the birds are singing in the trees. And I see you with a girl. The two of you are holding hands at the top of a hill overlooking an open field. But I also see storm clouds, a great loss, a perilous journey."

Alec was so taken aback he hardly knew what to say. It was as if Mrs. Pierce could read his mind. How could she know about Pam? How could she know that Pam and Alec had had a favorite place to sit together and watch the sunset back home at Hopeful Farm? It was a spot on a hill behind the barn overlooking the pastures, just as Mrs. Pierce had described.

To Alec, losing Pam was a private sadness he lived with daily. He rarely spoke about it to anyone, even to his friends, Henry or his parents. Yet this woman seemed to know all about it.

Mrs. Pierce gave him a deep stare, looking at him soulfully. Then, after a long moment, a smile flicked the corners of her mouth.

"Had you going, didn't I?" she clucked. "It's a stock reading. Fits everyone, good-looking young folks like you particularly. He-he-he. Who hasn't lost somebody they love? Not many, I guess."

"You had me going, all right," Alec said, "more than you know." He tried to regain his composure, surprised at himself that he could be taken in so easily.

Mrs. Pierce smiled, almost shyly. She seemed to sense Alec's lingering discomfort. "Don't feel too bad, lad. Most folks are easy to read. People are pretty much the same everywhere. Human fears and desires are all too common."

"So it's all just an act, then?" Alec asked.

She shrugged and took another sip of coffee. "Oh, most of it is pure flimflam, sure," she said. "But not all. My mother really could read signs in nature sometimes, like when storms were coming, often days in advance, that sort of thing. I remember many a time when fishermen would consult her about the weather before shipping out for a long voyage. Ma said she could talk to the trees, but that you had to know how to listen, to understand them. They speak in a language you don't hear with your ears. It seems the trees have a different sense of time as well. They might not answer you back for a year or two, if ever.

"Aye, lad," she said finally. "Many of the women in my mother's family have had the gift. Some of us more than others." She smiled, her eyes sparkled mischievously. "I missed out, for the most part," she said. "I get feelings sometimes. Sometimes they're right. I don't know how. Tom and Bartley had me picking ponies for them once upon a time."

"How'd you do?" Alec asked.

She shrugged. "Not bad. I guess we about broke even in the end. Tom still asks my opinion on the subject once in a while. He thinks I have a kelpie whispering in my ear."

"I've heard about the kelpies," Alec said.

"Tom mentioned you were asking about them," she said. "I know it's hard to believe in such things, though if you live here long enough, you'll hear stories that will make you wonder. I remember one my ma used to tell. It happened not far from here, as a matter of fact."

"What happened?" Alec asked.

Mrs. Pierce stretched back in her chair. "The way I heard it," she said, "a boy and his sister were out swimming in a lake when they stumbled upon a white horse drinking water from a stream nearby. All tacked up, he was, in the finest leather and silver. The children assumed the horse belonged to some wealthy Traveler. They waited for the man, but when no one showed up, the girl climbed up into the saddle, just to see what it was like to be seated on such a fine horse. The horse seemed friendly at first. But when she tried to get down, she couldn't lift herself out of the saddle. The horse suddenly burst into a mad gallop and carried the girl off."

Mrs. Pierce paused a moment for dramatic effect. Light sparkled in her eyes. "And then, what should the boy see but the white horse splashing out into the water. It swam out into the deep water and then dove beneath the surface, taking the screaming girl with it. Neither the girl nor the horse was ever seen again, alive or dead."

"And that was the end of it?" Alec asked.

Mrs. Pierce shook her head. "Not at all, lad. Why, to this day some folks say that out on the lake, no matter how cold it gets, there is a dark spot that never freezes. And when the wind blows just so, they say you can hear what sounds like the cries and sobs of a girl calling up from the bottom of the lake."

Alec started to speak. Mrs. Pierce raised her hand, signaling him to wait. "Aye, I know what you are thinking. 'Tis naught but a yarn to beguile the gullible. And well it might be. I've never been to the lake myself, so I can't really say for sure."

"Actually, I wasn't going to say that at all," Alec said. "In fact, I could swear that something very much like that happened to me."

"Tell me about it," she said.

Alec described his encounter with the ghostly horse and rider on the beach last month. "But that wasn't in Ireland," Alec said finally. "It was Long Island, only a couple hours from New York City."

"Maybe a kelpie swam over for a visit," Mrs. Pierce said.

Alec shrugged. "I was half asleep," he said. "I

figure I must have been dreaming. At the time, it was certainly unnerving, though. Are the kelpies always supposed to be bad?"

"Usually," she said, "but not always. Ma told another story about a boy who was walking the beach after a storm and found a horse with its legs tangled in a fishnet. When the boy freed the horse, it ran off. The boy followed the tracks up the beach until they led straight into the sea. At that very spot the boy found a pearl the size of an almond in the sand at the water's edge."

Mrs. Pierce smiled and picked up Alec's cup and idly examined the insides again.

"Anything there about the future?" Alec asked.

She smiled. "Looks good to me. Adventure. Love. Travel. Whatever you want, lad."

That evening, Alec took a walk out to the pasture after dinner. He was the only one at the farm besides the horses at the moment. With Bartley gone, Alec inherited the task of bringing them in from their pastures and back to the barn for the night.

After visiting awhile with the Black, Alec strolled over to the next pasture, a wide green field that ran all the way to a headland overlooking the sea. Along the way he passed the place Tom had called a fairy ring, something he called a "cromlech," a spot where a half-dozen flat, lichen-covered stones were formed into a circle. Tom had pointed it out when they'd taken a quick tour of the farm on Alec's second day here.

"There are circles of stone half buried in the earth all over Ireland," Tom had said, "all left there by farmers too superstitious to move them. No one's really certain of their true purpose, only that they date back to Irish prehistory. Legend had it that the unwary could fall into a fairy ring and never return."

Alec remembered Tom's words and looked across the field. A soft wind blew over him, the tall grass and the silent, tilting stones. There did seem to be something magical about this place above the cliff, Alec thought. And there was certainly a spectacular view of the coast from here, all the way to what looked like the towers of a ruined castle far in the distance.

Off toward the middle of the sprawling pasture, Alec could see the pony grazing with the Irish hunters. He had an apple in his pocket and called to the gray. Silver raised his head, whinnied and walked over to where Alec was standing. Alec pulled the apple out of his pocket and held it out to the pony. Silver bit half and, as unlikely as it seemed for the treat-happy pony, modestly spit the other half back into Alec's hand.

The pony walked off a short way but, upon seeing Alec wasn't following, turned back, beckoning with his head over his left shoulder.

"Hey, where you going?" Alec called as Silver

wandered out to the edge of the cliff. "Don't you want the rest of your apple?" Silver kept on walking and Alec followed him through the pasture to a place where some fallen rails made a gap in the fence. Here the pony approached Alec again, took the other half of the apple in his mouth and then very deliberately nudged Alec with his nose, turning him around to see the sunset.

The sight before him took Alec's breath away. The entire sky seemed to be on fire. For the next few minutes all he could do was stand there and watch spellbound as the show of blushing colors in the sky transited from light to dark. To Alec, it looked as if the sky was changing to every color imaginable. It was a glorious sight and he felt privileged to be here to witness it.

Alec was so caught up in the light show that he barely noticed it when Silver nudged him from behind again. When the pony bumped him yet again, Alec just had time to catch himself from tumbling forward. "Easy, boy," Alec said. "You don't want to push me over the edge of the cliff, do you? Who's going to bring you apples then, huh?"

Silver tossed his head and snorted. To Alec's astonishment, he saw a startling look flash through the pony's eyes, not a pleading for more goodies but a dark, malevolent, frightening look that would have been more appropriate in a predator stalking its prey. Alec tried to squeeze by to higher ground when the pony cut him off, blocking his way.

"Stop it, would you?" Alec said. "This is no place to be playing around." Silver didn't move, just stood there staring at Alec. His eyes were bright with mischief and malice, like a cat's eyes when toying with a mouse.

Alec was stunned. Could the pony really be trying to back him over the edge of the cliff? Alec tried to step around the pony, but once again Silver blocked his way. The pony swung his head. His back and neck arched aggressively, his nostrils flared. He stepped forward, pushing Alec toward the three-hundred-yard drop to the sea below.

"Whoa," Alec called sharply, but the pony wouldn't stop. Inching ahead, Silver maneuvered Alec closer and closer to the edge of the cliff. "Get back!" Alec called, waving his arms. Silver ignored him and pressed forward.

Shifting his weight onto the balls of his feet, Alec faked to the left and then pivoted to the right. His quick two-step maneuver caught Silver flat-footed, allowing Alec to slip around him and climb to higher ground.

"What is with you?" Alec called out, his heart racing. Silver did not move. Finally the pony turned and stepped away from the edge of the cliff. Again Alec looked at the pony. Silver blinked and stared back, the look in his eyes completely different now, his eyelids drooping as if he were half asleep and dreaming.

After a moment Silver shyly sidled closer and pressed his nose against Alec's shoulder. He began nudging Alec's pockets, looking for more treats as if nothing had happened. "Enough," Alec said, pushing him away. Silver pushed back, gently pressing his muzzle against Alec's palm to lick the salt from his hand and wrist.

What in the world provoked that malevolent light in Silver's eyes only a few moments before? Alec wondered. Perhaps it had never really been there. Perhaps he'd misread the whole thing and the pony was just nudging his jacket trying to find another apple. Or maybe he wanted to go back to the barn. Maybe it was all completely innocent.

Alec continued stroking the pony's soft neck and then took hold of the halter. "Easy now," he said. "I know, I know. Come on now." The pony obeyed him willingly, but as Alec walked him back to the gap in the fence, he couldn't help but wonder what Silver was really thinking.

14

THE KING KELPIE

AFTER REPLACING THE fallen-down fence rails, Alec brought the Black, Silver and the rest of the horses down to the barn for the night. He went inside the house, and, as he was sitting down to eat, the phone began to ring. Alec answered and Bartley was on the other end of the line. He said the organizers of the Old Fair Day celebration that weekend were planning a traditional Irish horse race through the countryside and across the Oorloch Strand and that they'd be honored if Alec would participate as a guest monitor for the race.

"The race is open only to local horses," Bartley said, "really just an excuse for the resident equestrians to get together and have some fun." He added that there was a first-place prize of two hundred pounds, just to keep things interesting.

Alec said he'd be glad to help out any way he could and agreed to meet with the officials the morning before the race. Hanging up the phone, he returned to the kitchen and his meal.

When Mora heard about the race, she responded as Alec thought she would and immediately made it clear she wanted to enter Silver, confident that the pony could win. It was assuming a lot, Alec knew, but he also knew he would probably feel the same way if he were in her shoes. Everyone needed dreams, didn't they?

Another day passed and still no one came to claim the pony. Mora spent much of the time with Silver down at the beach. The pony was once again acting as mild-mannered as ever. There were no more signs of what-ever it was that seemed to have possessed him that afternoon on the cliff. Certainly the pony had only been nudging Alec's pockets looking for treats. He did mention the incident to Mora and warned her about spoiling the pony with too much hand feeding. They didn't want to turn him into a beggar.

That afternoon, as Mora and Alec were standing by the fence in Silver's pasture, they heard the sound of a car engine coming up the driveway.

"It's my dad," Mora said.

"How can you tell?" Alec asked. "I can't see any-thing."

"Nothing else could sound like that old clunker of his." A second later an old, wood-paneled station wagon came into view and coughed to a stop by the barn. Two people got out, a man and a woman.

"He brought Aunt Sharon too," she said. Mora called and waved, then ran over to meet them. Silver tagged along behind her and Alec followed also.

"So that is the famous Silver," the woman said as they approached. She was wearing a blue suit and a hat. There was a little gray showing at the sides of her shiny black hair.

Mora introduced them. "This is my dad and my aunt Sharon," she said.

The man stepped forward to shake Alec's hand. "Pleased to meet you, Alec," he said. "Ryan Bolger." He was a rugged-looking, thickset man with a walrus mustache and short blond hair, suntanned and forty-something. The woman offered her hand next. She was slimmer than her brother, with a friendly face.

The Black whinnied from his adjoining pasture and sprang into a canter across the grass, stopping only when he reached the fence. "That's the Black, Dad," Mora said.

"He's showing off for you," Alec said.

"I've been hearing about that horse of yours around town," Aunt Sharon said. "Wasn't he injured in a race or something?"

"Not badly," Alec said. "Just a bruise. He's better

now. The seawater here is a great therapy. Exactly what he needed."

"I'm sorry that we haven't spoken sooner," Mr. Bolger said, "but you know how it is. With the lousy fishing these days we're working harder than ever and still can't fill our nets." They talked some more, and, after Mora walked her aunt down to take a look at the barn, Mr. Bolger confided that he'd been feeling guilty about spending so much time away from his daughter. He said he was glad she had found something she liked to do besides wander the beach by herself. "She always was a wee bit shy, that one."

"I noticed that," Alec said.

"She'll be going back to her mother's soon," her dad said. "I imagine she'll be glad to see her friends."

"Sure she will," Alec said. "That pony is giving her plenty of company in the meantime."

"Wish we could afford to get her a pony of her own," Mr. Bolger said. "Right now, I just don't know if it's in the cards. I suppose we'll see."

Alec nodded sympathetically.

"But what I really wanted to talk about," Mora's dad said, "is this race. The girl is all on about it. Do you think it's safe?"

"Race riding is always risky," Alec said. "That's why we wear helmets."

"She has her heart set on it," Mr. Bolger said. "I hate to disappoint her. My question to you is: Do you think she is up to it?"

"Mora's not a bad rider," Alec said honestly. "She has a good, natural seat and can handle a fast gallop as well as any kid I've ever seen. The pony took off with her on the beach the other day and she hung on like a pro. Some of her general horse sense isn't all it could be. At times I think the pony is calling the shots more than she is. But to answer your question, yes, I'd say she is up to it. She's inexperienced, but I wouldn't stop her from riding in a friendly race because of any lack of ability on her part. That said, anything can happen in a horse race, even a friendly one."

"Of course," Mora's dad said. "I just wanted your opinion, as a professional horseman."

"She seems competent to me," Alec said. "I don't know what more I can say."

Mr. Bolger nodded and smiled. "I hear that she won't be the first youngster to ride in the race. A girl younger than Mora came in second last year, I believe. I just wish I could be there to see it," he said with a sigh. "Unfortunately, I'll be shipping out early tomorrow morning. The trip will keep me away from home for a couple days at least. Sharon will be there, though, to head up the cheering section."

They met Mora and her aunt and walked together back to their car. Alec thanked them for stopping by. After they'd gone, Bartley put Mora to work raking up and sweeping out the barn aisle. Silver munched hay in his paddock. Alec walked out to the Black's pasture to check on him.

Mora's folks seemed like good, salt-of-the-earth people, Alec thought as he made his way along the path to the Black's pasture. He tried to imagine what it would be like working on a fishing boat for days at a time, like Mora's dad. Certainly it wasn't an easy way to make a living.

Alec slipped through the gate and out to where the stallion was grazing in the shade of a tree. The stallion nickered low and gladly at the sight of him. "Good boy," Alec said, patting the dark velvet cheek.

The Black glanced at Alec, a searching intelligence in his eyes. Then the stallion suddenly raised his head, disdainful and high, his neck an arc of arrogance. The Black back-stepped away and began prancing back and forth impatiently.

"You want to play, is that it?" Alec asked. The Black spun around, loped over to one of the few patches of ground that wasn't covered in grass and lowered his bulk onto the dirt. A second later he was rolling over onto his back, grunting with pleasure.

Alec watched his horse lolling in the dirt and grass for a few more minutes, idly wondering how things were going back at Hopeful Farm and if he should give them a call later that evening. The Black stood up and paced around some more. He seemed restless, so Alec decided they should take a walk. Soon they were following the fence bordering the driveway. When they reached the road, Alec turned the stallion to the path to the beach.

As he and the Black made their way along the strand, Alec saw a figure standing on the beach near a bend in the shoreline. It was Mike Malloy, the wood-carving fisherman he'd met earlier.

"How's the fishing?" Alec asked him when they met.

The old fisherman shrugged. "Not so good. Found some nice pieces of driftwood, though." The Black gave a snort and tossed his head.

"Easy, boy," Alec said, turning him in a short circle and coming back to the fisherman again.

"Certainly a magnificent animal," Mr. Malloy said, "the very image of the King Kelpie himself."

"The King Kelpie?" Alec asked. "Who's that?"

"The king of the kelpies. One of our local legends hereabouts. Big beautiful horse that carries off anyone unwary enough to try to ride him."

"I've been hearing stories about kelpies," Alec said. "Supposed to live underwater. Like sea monsters or something."

"You got it," Mike said.

"I even thought I saw one once at a beach on Long Island."

"Maybe he swam over to the States for a visit."

Alec laughed. "I've heard that before too."

"Don't laugh too hard," Mike said testily. "The only thing a kelpie covets more than a beautiful young girl is a beautiful black horse like himself. Maybe he's got an eye on your friend here. Come to think of it, I thought I saw a kelpie down at the pub the other night."

"A horse?"

"No, of course not," Mike said. "The kelpie is a shape-shifter. He was in human guise that night, down at the end of the bar drinking a pint. Chasing after the local girls, he was. Dark-eyed gent with piece of sea-weed in his hair."

The fisherman gave Alec a wink and smiled. "But the local girls are up on the likes of 'im. Make no mis-take, the kelpie won't be fooling any of them with his foxy tricks."

"Seaweed in the hair?" Alec said. "Is that how you tell?"

"One way."

"Well, I'll keep a look out for that, then. But don't worry. We can take care of ourselves."

The fisherman smiled and looked up at the towering figure of the black stallion. "Just so much, lad. Just so much."

the stranger

ON FRIDAY AFTERNOON, the day before the race, Mora and Alec were sitting at a table on the back porch eating lunch. They were alone at the farm just then. Bartley was in Oorloch picking up barn supplies, and Mrs. Pierce was leaving for town to do some errands herself. Alec could still see her car puttering down the lane. Her old hound, Martin, was in the passenger seat, his head stuck out the window, his ears flopping in the breeze.

As Alec and Mora ate their sandwiches, Alec suddenly noticed someone walking up the driveway toward them.

"Looks like we have company," Alec said.

The man walked closer. He was a pale, slender figure, not tall but military in bearing. Under one arm he carried a heavy-looking saddle. In his other hand was a bridle strung with tassels.

"Hallo," the man called, placing the tack on the porch steps. He had a young face and, except for the color of his long hair, a weird mixture of silver, white and blond, appeared to be in his late twenties or early thirties. His eyes were sunken, dark and colorless, almost opaque under silver-blond eyebrows. A black silk scarf was tucked around his neck and trailed over his shoulder.

"I'm looking for the Dailey farm." His voice was deep. The expression on his face was familiar and friendly, but his eyes remained dark and penetrating.

"You found it," Alec said.

"My name is Olivaros. Celestine Olivaros. Peace be with you."

Who was this guy? Alec wondered. Where was he from? Olivaros? Celestine? Those didn't sound like traditional Irish names. His accent wasn't Irish, more European sounding, perhaps upper-class Spanish or Portuguese.

The man held up a folded-back piece of newsprint in his hand. "I saw this notice in the newspaper," he said, "the one about the pony."

Mora stepped back behind Alec as the man explained that he'd lost the pony after a traffic accident. He said a car had collided with the horse-drawn trailer he was driving and landed him in the hospital for the past week.

"I'm sorry to hear that," Alec said.

Alec invited the man into the house. He introduced Mora and explained that she was the one who found the pony and was taking care of him.

Mora tried to smile, but Alec could see she was having a hard time hiding her feelings. Over the past few days she'd been making big plans for herself and Silver and had just about talked herself out of believing anyone would ever show up to claim him. Now it looked as if all her plans were falling apart and Alec could see the disappointment in her eyes.

The man looked around the room, shifting on his feet uneasily, like someone not used to being indoors. His bright, black eyes darted one way and then another under his thin, angular brows. It was as if he wanted to be sure where to find the doors in case he needed to make a quick exit.

"With my trailer still in the shop," Olivaros said, "I'd be obliged to you if the pony could stay here a bit longer, just until I can get us on the road again. Shouldn't be more than a few more days. Of course, I can pay whatever you think is fair for his room and board then."

"You can work that out with Mr. Dailey when he returns," Alec said. "Or Bartley. He's the stable manager. Neither is here at the moment. We're really just guests ourselves." He tilted his head to where Mora had been standing a moment ago, but she wasn't there now.

Alec glanced around the room. "Now where did she get off to? Oh, I know. Probably went out to the barn to get Silver. She calls the pony Silver."

Olivaros's eyes flashed and he stepped quickly toward the door and glanced outside, as if looking for someone. He jerked his head suddenly, and, as he did, his scarf fell from his neck. Before he replaced it, Alec glimpsed a pair of deep, purple scars on the man's neck.

That there were marks on the man's neck was not so startling all in itself. It was the shapes that drew Alec's attention, the exact same crescent shapes as the marks on Silver's neck. Olivaros turned his attention from the door to face Alec again.

Alec tried not to stare at the scarf around the man's neck. "Mora's done a good job with your pony," he said. "They've grown quite attached to each other."

"I'll have to think of a way to thank her properly for her help," Olivaros said.

"She was really looking forward to riding him in that race tomorrow," Alec offered hopefully.

The dark-eyed man smiled. "Oh, I don't see any reason why she shouldn't ride in the race if she wants. And, like I said before, I'm not quite ready to take her—I mean him. Not just yet."

"I know she'll appreciate it," Alec said.

The man gave a nod and a slight, cordial bow. "I'd be honored. And please feel free to use my saddle and bridle. It's the least I can do for all your kindness."

"Very nice of you," Alec said. "Silver has been a pleasure to work with."

"He's a good pony," Olivaros said, "but I think I'd sell him to a good home if I could find one. Traveling the roads by horse caravan is simply getting too dangerous for me. One hundred pounds would do nicely."

"Mora would take you up on the offer in a heartbeat if she had the money," Alec said. "But I don't think the kid has five pounds, much less a hundred. Anyhow, I'll tell her what you said."

Olivaros shook his head. "Times are hard all over," he said sympathetically.

There was a sudden rush of footsteps on the walk outside and Mora burst into the room. "He's gone," she cried. "Silver's not in his stall."

"What?" Alec said. "Are you sure?"

"Of course I'm sure."

"He's not out in the pasture?"

She shook her head. "Why would he be there? You saw me put him in his stall yourself."

"Come on," Alec said as he started for the door.

Alec and Mora rushed outside and over to the barn. Silver's stall was indeed empty. They checked the other wing of the barn and found no sign of him there either.

"He must be outside," Alec said. But when they looked in the pasture behind the barn, the pony was nowhere in sight.

Mora slipped through the fence railing and ran over to a small rise where she could see all the way to the far pasture. She stood there a moment, shielding her eyes with her hands. Finally she waved back to Alec.

"There he is," she called.

Alec climbed over the fence and ran up the rise to see for himself. "I'll get him," Mora said before Alec could reach her.

"Hey," Alec called after her. "He's not going anywhere this minute. You don't need to . . ." But by then Mora was beyond hearing, or stopping.

Atop the rise in the pasture Alec could see the pony out by the fence overlooking the cliff at the far end of the upper pasture. How in the world did he get out there? Alec wondered.

He took a deep breath and watched Mora chase out to her pony. Poor kid, Alec thought. Her dream of keeping Silver was going up in smoke. He couldn't help but feel a little sorry for her just then.

Turning around, Alec started back toward the barn, wondering what had happened to their visitor. He looked over to the house but could see no sign of

Olivaros there. Perhaps the man had followed them to the barn, Alec thought. He walked down to the barn and looked inside. Other than the horses, there was no one there either. Alec circled to the other side of the barn, where he found Mora riding the pony down from the pasture and into the paddock.

"The pony doesn't have to go back in his stall just yet," Alec said. "He may as well stay outside, as long as he's out here."

Mora gave a heavy sigh. By her gloomy expression Alec could tell that the fact that her days with the pony were numbered was beginning to sink in.

"Mr. Olivaros said you could still ride Silver in the race tomorrow," Alec said, trying to cheer her up a bit. He also mentioned the man's offer to sell the pony for a hundred pounds.

Mora's face brightened. "Really?"

"That's what he told me," Alec said.

"If I could only get the money somehow," Mora said. "I know my dad and Aunt Sharon would lend me the money, if they had it." Her expression turned downcast again. "But the way things are . . . I think we are barely scraping by as it is."

Alec gave the girl a consoling pat on the back. "At least you'll get to ride Silver in the race."

"Yeah, but after that . . . he'll be gone forever."

They stood there a moment in silence. And then,

suddenly, a light went on in Mora's eyes. "Unless," she said, "unless we win the race. Isn't there a two-hundred-pound prize to the winning rider? If I win, I could buy Silver with the prize money and have a hundred pounds left over."

"You never know with horse racing," Alec said, though he again wondered about the wisdom of getting Mora's hopes up.

"Silver is fast for his size."

"Sure," Alec said, "but he'll be racing against bigger horses with longer legs."

"He can do it," Mora said firmly, her eyes shining with determination. "He stayed with the Black when we raced the other day, didn't he?"

"That was over a short distance," Alec said. "This will be a real race over a distance of miles."

"He can do it," Mora said, her voice determined. "I know he can."

Alec smiled, admiring the girl's confident words in spite of the odds against her. If Mora thought she could win the race, it wasn't his job to dash her high hopes. "Maybe you're right," he said. "Anything can happen in a horse race, especially in cross-country races. A lot depends on the terrain, how sharp the turns and long the straights. Over short distances a good quarter horse will outrun a Thoroughbred almost every time."

Mora looked over her shoulder back to the house. "So what happened to Mr. Olivaros?" she asked.

Alec shrugged. "I was wondering that myself," he said. "He's not in the barn. He must still be up at the house."

They walked around to the back porch but found no one there. The man wasn't in the house either. "This is really strange," Alec said. "Where could he have gone?"

Mora walked over to the porch steps and crouched down to look at the saddle. "Hey, look at this. There's a note." She passed it to Alec, who unfolded the piece of paper and read the words printed there in big block letters:

Pardon me for rushing off but I'm on foot and my ride wouldn't wait. I will be in touch later. Good luck at the race tomorrow. Maybe I'll see you there.

—Olivaros

Alec looked at Mora. "Ride?" he said. "What ride? I didn't see anyone drive by."

"Me either," Mora said.

Alec couldn't understand it. "Just like that he ups and leaves?"

Mora shook her head. "That guy is weird."

Alec shrugged. "I can't argue with you there," he said, and began to examine the ornamented saddle. It was surprisingly light for its size, certainly not too much weight for the burly little pony. It had a deep seat, a high cantle and pommel, almost like a silver-studded Mexican saddle, only studded with pearl-like shells instead of silver. The saddle strings were beaded with tiny shell-shaped silver bells and more pearls. Alec reached down and fingered the leather. It felt used but well cared for. As far as Alec knew it wasn't really a traditional Irish outfit, though it certainly looked unique, to say the least.

Mora picked up the bridle. "Wow, look at that," she said. "This thing must be really old." She held up the bridle so Alec could see the circular, half-moon and crescent designs inlaying the nose band and brow band. Like the saddle, the inlay was of glossy white and pink mother-of-pearl. The pearls were set in a black leather background, making them shine like fire opals in the sunlight.

"It looks like the phases of the moon," she said.

"Come on," Alec said. "Let's take this tack down to the barn. We'll find some saddle soap and get to work on it."

BLOOD AND PEARLS

SOON ALEC HEARD a car rumbling up the driveway. A minute later Bartley walked into the barn. "Just had word from our renters when I was in town," Bartley said. "They seem to be getting along with our horses well enough. They want to keep them for another few days."

"Tom will be glad to hear that," Alec said. He told Bartley about the visit of the man who had come looking for Silver that afternoon.

"Did he show you any vet records or ownership papers?" Bartley asked. "How do you know he is telling the truth?"

"The man described the pony down to a tee," Alec said. "And there was something else too. You know the crescent-shaped scars on the pony's neck? They must be a clan sign or a family brand of some kind, a tattoo or something. I saw marks just like them on the guy's neck as well, two crescents spaced about an inch apart. The marks were shaped exactly the same as the ones on the pony's neck."

"That's a bit odd," Bartley said. "Are you sure?"

"They certainly looked the same to me," Alec said. Bartley listened as Alec described the stranger with the shadowy eyes and recounted the man's story of being stuck in the hospital for the last week after a car sideswiped his horse-drawn trailer.

"Sounds like a Traveler," Bartley said, "except for the Spanish surname."

Alec remembered the cart horses he'd seen hitched to the parked trailer during the drive from the race-track. It wasn't easy picturing Silver pulling a trailer like that, Alec thought. Again it made him wonder about Mr. Olivaros and whether or not the man's claim to the pony was genuine. Maybe Olivaros wasn't a Traveler at all. The chances were a million to one that the matching crescent-shaped marks were simply some sort of coincidence, but you could never tell. Maybe Olivaros had seen the notice in the paper and was trying to bluff his way into a free horse.

Come to think of it, Alec thought, he hadn't seen the gypsy and the pony together, so he couldn't even judge if the pony recognized this supposed owner or not. It would be something to watch for the next time they met. And, Alec decided, it wouldn't hurt to ask to see some sort of proof of ownership before he turned the pony over to Olivaros.

"What did he look like?" Bartley asked.

Alec recalled the man vividly. "He had very pale skin," Alec said, "thin red lips, long, silvery white-blond hair and beard; even his eyebrows looked silver-blond. Now that I think about it, the only thing dark about him was his eyes. They seemed almost black. I suppose it was because the rest of him was so light-colored."

Bartley scratched his chin. "Pale skin?" he said. "That's not something I would have expected. Travelers tend to have darker skin than your typical Irishman."

"Not this guy," Alec said. "His was practically like an albino's."

Bartley walked over to the tack room, saying he had chores to do. Mora asked if she could help and Bartley was happy to oblige her.

"Why don't you walk into town and see what's doing at the fair, Alec?" Bartley suggested. "Enjoy yourself for a change."

"Maybe I will," Alec said. He walked outside to visit with his horse awhile, then decided to take Bartley's advice and stroll into town to check out the action at the fair.

Nearing the outskirts of town, Alec looked across to the harbor of Oorloch and the sea-ravaged coastline beyond. In his mind, he tried to picture what this wild, lonely place must have looked like a hundred years ago, before the automobile, when horses still ruled the roads—aside from the long, narrow, two-lane strip of pavement beside him, probably not much different than it did now.

Soon the breeze began to carry the sounds of soft music. Following the sounds, he came to a field behind the local firehouse. People milled around two long sheds and a dozen smaller stands and tents. The tantalizing aroma of barbecue floated in the air. A crowd was gathered around a little stage outside one of the open-walled tents. Alec made his way closer to the stage, where a fiddler was playing softly, his eyes closed. Beside him a young woman in a high-neck sweater sang a slow, mournful ballad about a fisherman lost at sea during a storm. The crowd watched quietly and then joined in with the chorus, something about "the gone but not forgotten." It was a sad song, Alec thought, about death and lost love, yet seemed perfectly suited for this place, as if inspired by the wild, windswept coast surrounding Oorloch.

After a few minutes, Alec threaded his way through the crowd, a mix of families, farmers, older folks and lots of kids, many around Mora's age. Inside one of the long sheds he saw displays of blue-ribbon varieties of local produce, hay and grain, vegetables and honey-combs. In the other were cattle, chickens and sheep. Outside, vendors sold socks, gates and radios. Dogs barked; a goat butted the sideboard of a cart. A man wearing a jaunty riding cap and licking ice cream sat on a parked tractor.

Some of the food stands sold cakes and pies, others traditional Irish fare like corned beef and cabbage and fish and chips. Alec noticed that a few stands offered not-so-traditional Chinese dumplings and East Indian curries. A group of young men stood around an open fire pit roasting a pig on a spit.

The sight and smell of all the food was starting to make Alec hungry, so he lined up at one of the stands to buy something to eat. A girl with copper-colored hair fixed him an order of fresh fish and chips.

The picnic tables were crowded and it took Alec a moment to find a place to sit down to eat. Beside him, two leather-faced old-timers clutched paper cups of steaming tea and spoke in low, almost whispered tones that Alec would never have heard if he hadn't been squeezed in beside them. He ate his food as the men talked of the unusually dry weather, of the sorry state of fishing these days, of just exactly where the Gulf Stream reached the shores of Ireland.

Over on the bandstand, a guitar player and a

bagpiper joined the group onstage. Soon the band was playing a lively tune that, to Alec, sounded almost like American bluegrass music, a showy instrumental reel.

Alec finished his meal, then walked around to the other side of the bandstand and past the small Ferris wheel, all decked out with blinking green and yellow lights. He could hear screeches coming from another ride that looked like a giant metal octopus swinging riders about in a frenzy. Popping sounds came from an air-rifle shooting gallery, where Alec saw a row of teddy bears on the prize racks and live goldfish swimming inside little glass bowls.

He edged his way through the crowd, finally strolling over to the empty race tent where a gold-colored banner read "The Oorloch Cup Challenge, Established 1888." Beyond the banner he could see the racecourse marked by a series of wooden stakes flagged with yellow ribbons placed every fifty yards or so.

Alec took another quick turn around the fair and then, as it was already late in the afternoon, decided he'd better be going home. He would see plenty more of the fair tomorrow and wanted to walk the course a ways if he could before dark. As it turned out, much of the course led in the same direction as the farm.

Following the yellow flags marking the course,

Alec passed through an open field to a wide country lane that bordered a wooded area and then became a tunnel through the trees. From there the course curved across a shallow stream, continuing on through a low-lying glen, past the edge of a golf course, then over another stream to a dirt lane that ran along the dunes bordering the beach. Alec turned off the course there, but he could see the yellow flags marking the way to the beach, where the course curved back to town and the final stretch ran over the sand at the water's edge.

Mora was still hanging around the barn when Alec arrived back at the farm a few minutes later. Bartley's car was gone. Silver and the other horses were already bedded down for the night in their stalls. Only the Black remained outside, grazing alone in his pasture.

Alec walked up the barn aisle to where Mora sat on a trunk outside Silver's stall. At the moment she was intently giving Olivaros's saddle and bridle another going-over with saddle soap and a dry sponge. Again Alec couldn't help but admire the bridle's fine workmanship, its lustrous inlay of pearls, shells and tiny silver bells.

Alec nodded at the pony's stall. "Better give your buddy an extra ration of oats before bed tonight. He'll be skipping breakfast tomorrow, so this will be his last regular meal before his race."

Mora's eyes shone brightly as she worked over the saddle. "You ready for tomorrow?" Alec asked.

"Am I!" she said confidently. "We can win; I know we can. Silver is the fastest horse I've ever ridden."

"Maybe so," Alec said, "but he'll have plenty of competition. I gather the race is a pretty big deal around here."

"We can do it," she said. "We have to." Mora kept her eyes on her work as she spoke, buffing the leather saddle to a deep, glossy sheen.

"Everyone in town is getting geared up for the fair tomorrow," Alec said. "Most of the booths are already open."

"What's it like?" she asked.

"I saw some sheep and cows," Alec said. "And there is a band playing too. You might want to check it out on your way home."

"I guess I can wait until tomorrow," she said, looking up from her work finally. "I've seen cows and sheep before. I'm from Ohio, remember?"

Alec smiled and picked at the saddle strings hanging from the saddle Olivaros had left them, fingering the tiny bells and pearl-colored shells.

"Now that's something you don't see every day," he said. "Pearl-beaded saddle strings."

"They almost look real," Mora said.

"Who knows?" Alec said. "They very well could

be, especially on a one-of-a-kind saddle like this. And I wouldn't be surprised if the inlay on the brow band is real pearl either."

Mora gave the brow band another swipe with her sponge. The moon-shaped designs sparkled in the overhead light shining down from the rafters.

Alec touched the saddle and ran his fingers over the smooth, dark tan-colored leather. As he did he noticed a trail of dark splatters staining one of the saddle flaps. "Hey, look at this," he said.

"I tried to get that out," she said. "No way."

"Doesn't surprise me," Alec said. "It looks like blood."

"Do you think so?"

"Could be," Alec said. "Whatever it is, it looks like it's been there for a long time."

Mora stood up and looked to the open barn door. Outside, the remaining light of day was beginning to fade. "I was thinking I might take Silver for a quick ride before I go home."

"Sounds like a good idea," Alec said. "Why don't you give the new saddle and bridle a try and see how they feel? Better to find out now than tomorrow morning if you're not comfortable with them. If anything doesn't feel right you should probably use his old saddle for the race tomorrow."

Alec set to tacking up the pony and again he noticed

the surprising lightness of the saddle as he hefted it onto the pony's back. He was just centering the saddle when he felt a sharp, burning sensation shoot up his arm, like the sting of a wasp. The sudden shock was strong enough to knock him back and off his feet.

Mora ran over to him. "Hey," she cried. "You okay?"

Alec's arm still tingled as he looked up and saw Silver standing almost on top of him. The pony looked strangely different looming over him, and for a moment Alec's blurred vision told him this couldn't be the same horse. Alec climbed to his feet and wiped the dirt from the side of his face.

"What happened?" Mora asked.

"I don't know, but I just got a wicked sting from something," Alec said. "Maybe a wasp, but I didn't see one. Or it could have been some sort of static electricity." He dusted himself off and cautiously touched the saddle again. This time there was no shock and he was able to finish getting the pony tacked up.

Silver stood easy, yet Alec still sensed something unusual about the pony now, as if the very air around him was charged with electricity. He seemed puffed up, his muscles swollen, his coat pulled tighter to a suddenly more powerful frame.

Alec ran his hand over the pony's neck. The texture of Silver's coat felt coarse, as if the hair was standing on end. "Maybe you should wait a second," Alec said. "This boy is really up on his toes right now."

"I'll be okay," she said.

Alec watched Silver a minute, then finally cupped his hands and gave Mora a leg up. She settled easily into her seat and urged the pony into motion. Alec waited by the fence while she rode Silver in loopy figure eights around the paddock and made a quick circuit of one of the fenced pastures. Again Alec noticed how the pony was perking up under the fancy new saddle and tack, his stride short, quick but powerful, his attitude confident, almost insolent.

"Wow," Mora said when she returned to the paddock. "This saddle feels great. And the bridle fits him perfectly too. All I have to do is finger the reins the slightest bit and he responds immediately. It's like he knows what I'm going to do even before I do."

Mora dismounted and walked the pony back to the barn. "Hey," Alec said, following a few steps behind, "you've got something on the back of your pants." Mora reached around and pulled off a small dust ball, like a piece of cotton stuffing or a cobweb, which had somehow become stuck to the seat of her pants.

"Gross," she said. She crouched down and rubbed her hands in the grass to wipe the sticky strands of web off her fingers. "Where did that come from?"

"You must have brushed up against a spiderweb on a fence rail somewhere," Alec said.

"I didn't bump into any fences," Mora said. "At least I don't think so."

Alec laughed. "Maybe it will help keep you in the saddle. The stuff looks sticky enough."

"Yuck," Mora said.

17

the oorloch cup

WHEN ALEC OPENED the barn door the next morning, Mora was there waiting for him. She'd already brought Silver out of his stall. The pony stood quietly in the aisle beside her as she brushed out the swirls in his cloud-colored coat. He looked great after all Mora's attentions, Alec noticed. His white forelock and mane were carefully combed, fringing his head and neck like a waterfall of fine, silken threads. He seemed to know there was something special in the air this morning, holding his head high, his eyes gleaming with pride, like a movie star preened for his big close-up.

Mora had dressed for the occasion and was wearing a new-looking blue sweater and neatly creased slacks. Her hair was tied back behind her head under her short-brimmed riding hat. As for Alec, he had borrowed one of Tom's suit jackets so he might look more presentable in his position as an honorary race monitor.

He ran his hand over the pony's wide back and gave him a pat on the neck. "He looks good," Alec said. "You remembered to skip his breakfast this morning, didn't you?"

Mora nodded and smiled. "Yes," she said. "And he isn't too happy about that either."

"I suppose he could have a whiff of oats before we go," Alec said. "Just keep it light. Nothing more than a couple handfuls, okay?"

"Okay," Mora said. Alec left her there and strolled over to the other end of the barn to give the Black his breakfast. After that he took the stallion outside and turned him loose in the pasture so he could stretch his legs a bit before the trip to town.

Soon it was time to get the Black ready to go. Alec looked back toward the barn and saw Mora already had Silver tacked up and was leading him out to meet them. Alec slipped through the fence rails and whistled to the Black, who was grazing beneath a tree on the far side of the green field. The stallion raised his head and began loping toward him. The big horse slowed as he came closer, tossing his head as if he sniffed something in the wind.

All at once, the Black froze in step, becoming completely motionless, rigid and suspicious. His eyes flashed with a combination of anger, hate and fear. The stallion backed up a step, then whirled and spun around.

The whites of his eyes shone brightly, now rimmed with fire. His nostrils were dilated and crimson.

Alec glanced over his shoulder to see what was provoking the stallion's sudden rage. All he could see was Mora standing beside Silver on the other side of the fence a dozen feet away. Turning to face the Black again, Alec saw the stallion step closer, then lunge at Silver, his teeth bared.

The Black's attack was swift and deadly, as if survival itself depended on the immediate destruction of his enemy. Alec threw up his hands. He moved with the Black, twisting his body like a matador as the stallion rushed past him. The Black charged the short distance to the fence, rearing to a stop just before crashing into the rails.

Outside the fence, Silver pulled Mora into a half circle. For some unexplainable reason the pony didn't seem to be frightened in the least and did not try to run away from the raging stallion. Only a few wooden rails stood between the two horses, but Silver seemed unconcerned, as if he knew the stallion's hooves could not touch him.

The Black reared again and pawed the air. "Get back," Alec shouted to Mora. "Get that pony out of here!"

Mora pulled frantically on Silver's lead. At first the pony stubbornly held his ground, unfazed by the

Black's display and Mora's futile attempts to pull him back. Finally he gave way and quietly followed her to the path and back to the barn, his long white tail swishing lightly behind him like one last taunt to the Black. Watching them go, the Black screamed his defiant screams and pawed the air. He paced back and forth next to the fence, trembling with fury, stopping only to beat the ground with his hooves in frustration.

Alec knew there was little he could do when the Black worked himself into a state like this. He waited for the fury to pass, and when the time was right he moved directly in front of the stallion. Facing the Black, he spoke to his horse, his voice firm and as calm as he could make it. "Easy now. Easy, boy," he repeated over and over.

Another minute passed before Alec drew closer to the stallion. The Black snorted but remained still. Alec let his hand go forward to the Black's mane, resting it there as it had rested a thousand times before. His voice dropped even softer. After a moment he laid his other hand on the Black's shoulder. The Black pulled back. Alec stepped with him and could feel the tremors of rage that still rippled the stallion's ebony coat.

"That's a boy," Alec whispered. "Easy now." The Black dropped his head low and close to Alec's shoulder, and Alec was left to wonder what had sparked off the stallion's fury a moment ago. He could only feel lucky the Black hadn't tried to jump the fence, or bull his way through it. Alec slipped the halter over the stallion's ears and attached the lead line. A moment later he was walking the Black along the fence in slow circles.

Somehow Alec just couldn't believe that the focus of all the Black's sudden fury was Silver. Certainly a pony like Silver was no threat to the stallion.

A few minutes later Mora came walking back to the pasture. Alec was glad to see she'd left Silver back at the barn this time. She made a sign to Alec and he waved her closer. Mora cautiously stepped up to the fence. The Black glanced at her suspiciously but did not seem overly concerned about her now. "What was that all about?" Mora asked.

Alec eased the Black to a stop. "Something really spooked the Black," he said. "I don't know what it is, but, believe me, I'm not taking him into town or any-where else right now. He's staying here."

Mora nodded her head. "That was really scary," she said. "It looked like he wanted to take Silver's head off all of a sudden."

"I know," Alec said. "I can't understand it either."

After a minute's discussion it was decided that Mora should take Silver and go ahead to the fair with-out him. Alec said he might be able to slip away and join her later, if he felt certain the Black had really shaken off whatever was bothering him.

"You better get going," Alec said. "You don't want to miss your race."

Mora nodded at the Black. "You sure he is okay now?"

"He's fine," Alec said. "Are you okay?"

"I wish you were coming with me."

"I'll be there if I can," Alec said.

Mora hesitated a moment, then turned and ran back to the barn. A minute later Alec saw her walking Silver up the driveway, headed for town. Once they were out of sight, Alec removed the Black's halter and turned the stallion loose.

The Black bucked and bounced a minute, but it seemed to be all in play. Soon the stallion set to grazing. Alec waited awhile longer and then, looking at his watch, decided he could still catch the race if he hurried. Before he left, he stopped by the barn to tell Bartley what he was doing. Bartley said he would keep an eye on the Black while Alec was in town.

With less than an hour to go before the start, Alec set off, jogging up the lane, slowing only to a walk when he was well on his way to town. The exercise felt good, especially here on this beautiful Saturday morning on the west coast of Ireland. The sun was shining with only a few high puffy clouds dotting the sky. The weather certainly has been nice for my stay here, he thought. There had been plenty of sun and it rained only a few times. Alec knew Ireland was famous for its wet and rainy climate as much as for its velvet green fields. He felt lucky for the fine weather that had blessed his trip so far.

There was more traffic than usual today and Alec kept to the side as the cars drove past on the narrow, two-lane road. He walked along, wondering what the race officials would say when they saw the Black wasn't with him. He might not be the most effective race monitor on foot, Alec knew, especially if all the other monitors were to be on horseback. Anyway, he would do the best he could.

Soon he was climbing up the hill behind the fire-house. Multicolored flags planted at the top of the hill were rippling in the offshore breeze. Down below, in a park on the other side of the low hill, the fair was in full swing. By the time he arrived, most of the horses were already waiting in the paddock area fenced off next to the official race tent. The Oorloch Cup, really a large silver bowl, sat like a chalice on a wooden podium outside the tent. It listed the engraved names of past winners going back one hundred years and more.

Alec checked in at the officials' desk, where a tall,

middle-aged woman wearing shiny black boots and riding pants introduced herself as Mrs. Featherstone of the racing steward's committee. Alec made his excuses for the Black's not being there. She said she understood completely, and that, even on foot, he could help monitor the start of the race from the sidelines.

Mrs. Featherstone showed Alec where he could pick up a fluorescent orange armband that would identify him as a race monitor for the start. She explained that other monitors would be positioned on horseback at half-mile marks the length of the course.

The monitors were to watch for any intentional interference, she said, something that they'd had trouble with in the past. If there were objections after the race, the monitors would be called on to bear witness before the stewards ruled on the final results. It was always a friendly race, Mrs. Featherstone explained, but many of the locals took it very seriously, as it ensured bragging rights for the year to come.

Alec thanked Mrs. Featherstone, put on his armband and walked over to the enclosure area that was serving as race paddock. Mora had taken up her place there, waiting for the call to the post with the dozen other horses and their riders. Most of the runners were Irish hunters, a few of which looked like they could gallop for miles without breaking a sweat. Certainly

Silver would have his work cut out for him if he hoped to keep pace with this group, Alec thought.

Alec waved to Mora and made his way to where she stood beside Silver, off to the side of the group and by themselves. The pony stood quietly watching the other horses, his ears pricked, wriggling the bit in his mouth. He looked terrific, as if he'd grown a couple of inches and put on pounds of muscle overnight.

Mora smiled. "You're here," she said. "I didn't think you'd come."

"Where's your aunt?" Alec asked. He glanced out among the crowd that was starting to gather outside the paddock.

"I haven't seen her yet, but I'm sure she's around here somewhere," Mora said. "I haven't seen any sign of Mr. Olivaros either."

Alec shrugged. Mora reached up to adjust the strap on her riding hat. "Do I look okay?" she asked.

"Not to worry, pal," Alec said. "You look great and so does Silver." Alec caught sight of a woman walking toward them. "There's Mrs. Pierce," he said.

"And here comes Aunt Sharon too," Mora said. She waved the two women closer.

"Well, look at you," Aunt Sharon said. Silver bobbed his head and she cautiously backed away. "Never was much of a horse person myself," she said, "at least as far as riding is concerned. I like to stay close to the ground. They are beautiful animals. I'll give you that."

Mrs. Pierce nodded her head in agreement. "Fine for the young. These days I'll be keeping company with my dogs."

Aunt Sharon looked around at the other runners in the paddock. "I wish her father could be here. I know he's feeling bad about being away."

Mora smiled and watched shyly as a group of boys walked by snacking on candy from small paper bags. "You should hang around after the race," Alec said. "You might meet some people your own age."

Aunt Sharon smiled. "There's an idea," she said. "Maybe we can all get together and have a bite somewhere after the race. The food smells good enough."

From outside the race tent came the rat-a-tat-tat of a bugle calling the horses to line up for the race. Alec gave Mora a leg up into the saddle.

"I'll walk you to the start," he said. They started off, Silver prancing along regally and swinging his head from side to side, his eyes forward.

As Alec had guessed, with the call to the post the fair crowd was migrating en masse from the other exhibits to the racecourse sidelines to watch the start. There was still no sign of Olivaros among the spectators bunching around the start.

Alec turned to Mora and he could see the

nervousness in her eyes. "Don't worry so much, Mora," Alec said. "You'll do fine."

"Easy for you to say," Mora replied. "This is my first race."

Alec laughed. "I remember how it was my first time," he said. "Believe me, the worst part is over—the waiting around beforehand. Now all you have to do is ride."

"Oh yeah," she said. "Any last-minute advice?"

"Just stay clear of the others at the start," Alec said. "This course must be almost three miles long. You'll have plenty of time, so take it easy. Try to save something for the homestretch run along the beach, okay?"

"I will," Mora said.

As they made their way to join the other runners, two of the horses closest to Silver began stamping and snorting nervously. Alec held up his hand and Mora pulled Silver to a stop. He wanted to wait for the two horses to collect themselves, but the commotion quickly spread to the other runners waiting for the start. Soon they were all acting up. Some were bucking and throwing hooves; others were backing away when their riders tried to mount up, turning in circles, whinnying and carrying on. The lone exception was Silver, who remained completely calm and collected, standing still with a cold, bright light glinting in his eyes.

The pony swung his head to face Alec. He gave Alec a deep stare, then winked an eye and nickered softly. After a moment Silver turned his attention to the horses, holding his head disdainful and high, like a general surveying his nervous troops before battle.

The riders finally got their horses under control and made their way to the start. "Okay, pal," Alec said. "You're on your own from here on in."

Mora gave Alec a brave smile and eased Silver ahead to join the other runners lining up for the start. A photographer from the local newspaper stood by the sidelines with a camera on a tripod, preparing to catch the start.

Watching Silver step off toward the other runners, Alec noticed a splotchy patch of white on Mora's right pant leg. "Whoa there, Mora," he called to her. "Hold on a second."

Mora pulled up and turned as Alec caught up to her. "Hang on," he said. "You have something on your pants."

"What?" Mora said.

"You must have brushed into that spiderweb or whatever it is again," Alec said. "You don't want to get your picture taken with that stuff all over you." He leaned over and touched the white splotch on her dark slacks. Some of it stuck to his fingers. "Where does this stuff keep coming from?" he said.

"Gross," she said, wiping the patch of white web off her leg with her free hand.

"There, you got it," Alec said.

"Okay, okay," she said quickly.

"Go on now," Alec said.

Mora rode off to line up with the other horses for the race. Alec touched his fingers together, feeling the sticky, cotton candy–like goo and wondering how on earth she kept picking up that stuff.

"and they're off!"

THE RUNNERS MOVED into place at the start. Two men stretched a long piece of elastic ribbon between them and the horses spread out behind it. People called out to their favorites from the sidelines.

When the horses were all more or less lined up, one of the starters released his hold on the ribbon and it snapped away. A burst of light flashed from the photographer's camera. The crowd roared. Riders called to their mounts, urging them on. The runners rushed forward in a flying stampede. All the runners except one.

All except Silver.

The pony took two steps and bounced to a dead stop, then reared up on his hind legs. Mora was caught unprepared. She lost a stirrup and one rein, fell straight backward, but then miraculously saved herself. A gasp went up from the crowd as she slipped to one side like a trick rider, regained the saddle, slid, slipped again, fell backward again. Each time she managed to just save herself, reins flying free, stirrups still unrecovered, her hands deep in the tangles of Silver's mane.

Alec watched as Mora went sprawling all over her mount. Her eyes were wide, an expression of shock on her face, a look more surprised than frightened. Silver thrashed about wildly. He snaked out his neck and began rocking on his heels. His body swelled as if new muscles were rising up and bulging beneath his silver coat.

The other horses streaked away from Silver as he threw back his head and shrilled savagely, a cry that was as terrifying as it was out of place. Never in a million years would Alec have associated that sound with the pony he'd come to know as Silver. Yet there was something frighteningly familiar about the war cry. He'd heard it before, and suddenly he remembered where, on his first morning there when the Black bolted off down to the point.

The pack careened through the open field. Silver catapulted after them in sharp, short, frantic bursts. Mora was leaning down low on his neck now, her hands and arms dug deep into his flying mane.

Alec watched as Silver began closing the ten-length gap separating him from the rest of the runners. With every stride, the pony's small body leveled out and came on stronger. Beyond the runners, Alec could see the next flag and the monitor who was to pick up the horses for the next segment of the race, a wide lane that led into the woods. Silver drove closer to the other horses before they all disappeared into the shadows beneath the trees.

There was no way Silver was keeping up that pace for much longer, Alec knew. At the rate he was going he would surely burn out by the time they reached the halfway mark, even if Mora managed to hang on that far.

With all of his attention focused on Mora and Silver, Alec could only hope that none of the other riders claimed a foul at the start so he wouldn't have to admit to neglecting his job as race monitor. All he could be sure of was that no one went down, though it certainly looked like a close call for Mora there for a while. Apart from that, Alec had little idea how the start unfolded for the rest of the horses.

The crowd was leaving the start area now. Some were already gathering at the finish line on the beach past the wharf. Alec hurried down to join them so he could watch the final stretch run over the strand. He found a good place to stand on a low dune about fifty yards from the finish. An onshore breeze blew softly against his face, bringing with it the sharp smell of fish and brine.

Soon he could see the horses charging toward him along the shoreline. Three front-runners were wrestling for the lead, with the rest of the field strewn out behind them. Alec couldn't make out Silver's position, but it was plain to see he was not bunched among the leaders.

But then, from out of nowhere, a gray streak suddenly began closing in from behind. It was Silver. Alec could barely believe what he was seeing, but there it was. The pony was still in the race, driving along behind the three leaders, then moving inside them along the water's edge.

As the horses drew closer to the final furlong, one of the front-runners began to tire and Silver quickly overtook him. The remaining two leaders plunged forward, their riders pushing them for every last bit of speed in the final rush to the finish. A dark bay held the lead over a golden chestnut now running a length behind. Mora and Silver were less than a length back, in third.

Straining bodies rose and fell as they skipped over the beach, sand flying from their hooves. The horses swerved closer to the water, the chestnut moving up alongside the bay, leveling out in the run for the finish. Silver fought for running room on the inside as the big bay edged him down to where the waves washed over the beach. But Silver wouldn't relent. Finding another gear, the pony gathered himself to fight back with everything he had.

Stride for stride the three horses came, their hooves hammering the hard sand down by the water's edge. The sounds of their thundering drive for the finish mixed with the cries of the riders calling to their horses and the clamor from the crowd along the dunes urging them on.

The front-runners drew closer to the pair of black flags planted in the sand that marked the end of the race. Mora kept low over her horse and seemed completely focused on her riding. She barely moved on the pony's back as they drove to the finish. Silver's ears were back and flat against his head, his legs a spinning blur.

The leaders were so close to the water's edge now that a wave washed up onto the sand in front of them. Spray flew from the horses' hooves as they flew through the puddles left by the receding wash of water. Slowing the others slightly, the splash of water only seemed to spur Silver to even greater speed. This time the leaders could not fight him off. Silver pushed a nose in front of the bay just as they crossed between the flags marking the end of the race, the winner.

Alec cheered with the rest of the crowd. What a race! What a pony! And Mora. After that wild start, simply completing the race at all would have been an achievement today, much less a come-from-behind win in the final strides.

It took another minute for the last few runners to make their way across the line. Alec followed the

crowd back to the fair and the award ceremony outside the race tent. Soon everyone was pushing and
shoving closer to the winner's circle. A ring of police
and race monitors tried to keep them back.

Alec worked his way through the excited crowd.
Voices chimed in around him. "That's some pony,"
someone said. "I wish I had him."

"Him?" someone else said. "He's an outlaw. And
he's not even local. He should never have been entered
in the race."

"The pony won fair and square," said another.
"And that girl rode a great race, settled her horse and
got down to business."

"Aye, 'tis a rare talent to be able to calm a frightened horse with your hands like that."

"Frightened? That animal wasn't frightened. He
went nuts. He should have been disqualified."

"Ah, don't be a sore loser, Danny."

A voice came over the loudspeaker system announcing Medora Bolger and her horse, Silver, as the
winners of the Oorloch Cup. Alec snaked his way to
the front of the crowd and inside the winner's circle.
Mora sat still on Silver's back, speaking to the pony,
rubbing her hands up and down his neck to keep him
quiet. Alec stepped closer until he caught Mora's
attention. Her face was speckled with sand. He nodded
to her and took hold of Silver's bridle.

"Way to go, pal," he said. "You did it."

"Silver's the best pony anywhere," she said breathlessly.

Alec gave the pony a pat on the neck. "And you did a great job of riding him."

Mora wiped some of the sand from her face. "I could hardly see a thing the last quarter mile with all the sand and spray in my eyes." She smiled proudly as she dismounted, her face flushed.

Mrs. Featherstone and another race steward draped a blanket of wildflowers around Silver's wet neck. Next Mora posed for pictures holding the silver bowl and the check for the prize money, to the applause of the people gathered there.

Silver took it all in stride, relaxed, head held high and ears pricked. He was acting his old friendly self once again, a completely different horse from the one who had reared up at the start. Whatever the trouble had been, he seemed to have run it out of himself over the course of the race. The pony shoved his head against Alec's chest playfully. Alec gently rested his hand on Silver's forehead. "Come on," he said. "We should get him away from this crowd."

They led the pony to where Mrs. Pierce and Aunt Sharon were standing to one side of the crowd. "Lord help me," Aunt Sharon said. "I never would have believed it."

Mora rubbed the pony's neck. Silver stood still, head held high, bright eyes staring off toward the ocean.

"Isn't he fantastic?" Mora said.

Aunt Sharon shook her head. "I about had a heart attack when he reared up at the start."

Mrs. Pierce kept her eyes fixed on Silver. A worried expression crossed her face, as if her thoughts were suddenly drawn far away. Even Mora noticed it. "Isn't it great, Mrs. Pierce?" she said. "We won. Mrs. Pierce? You okay?"

The old woman staggered suddenly and took Aunt Sharon's arm for support.

"Whoa there," Aunt Sharon said. "You okay?"

Mrs. Pierce caught her breath and steadied herself. "Just had the strangest feeling," she said, wiping her forehead with her free hand, "like this all happened before somewhere. But that's impossible." The cloud of worry passed from her face. She smiled and laughed. "Silly me," she said. "Guess I'm not used to all this excitement. It's terrific, Mora. Congratulations."

Silver looked as if he was becoming bored with all the talking and standing around. He nudged Mora's hand for attention. Mora ran her hand over the light gray muzzle.

After a minute Mora pulled the two-hundred-pound check out of her pocket and looked at it again, as if to reassure herself it was real. "Isn't it great, Aunt Sharon?" she said excitedly. "Now, with the money, I'll be able to buy Silver. I just know it. Mr. Olivaros told Alec he'd sell Silver to me for a hundred pounds. Isn't that right, Alec?"

"Something like that," Alec said.

"I'll find a way to get him back home," Mora said, her voice filled with determination. "I'll work after school, get babysitting jobs, do house cleaning, do whatever I have to do. Somehow I'll earn the money to keep him."

"We'll have to talk with your father about it when he gets back," Aunt Sharon said. "I'm sure he wishes he were here. He'd be very proud of you, Medora. I know it."

They took a quick walk around the fair and treated themselves to samplings of appetizers at an Indian curry stand. It was good to see Mora so happy, Alec thought.

After they were done eating, Alec offered to take care of the pony for her, but Mora said she wanted to ride home on her own. She had to pick up her bike anyway. Mrs. Pierce said she could give Alec a lift back to the farm and Alec agreed.

Silver was nibbling at the blanket of flowers around his neck, so Mora pulled it off him and handed it to Alec. "Good idea," he said. "It'll be easier if we take the flowers back with us in the car." Mora said she'd follow along and be there in a few minutes.

Soon Alec and Mrs. Pierce were sitting quietly in her car, driving the short distance to the farm. It was plain to see something was bothering her. "Feeling okay?" he asked.

"Oh, it's nothing, just one of those funny feelings of mine. Been happening more and more lately. I must be getting old. Don't let it bother you; it's nothing. I shouldn't even mention it." She paused a moment and shook her head. "There just seems to be something about that girl's pony today," she said. "Something unusual."

"I'll say. He has the acceleration of a quarter horse and the staying power of a Thoroughbred."

"That's not what I'm talking about. There is a look in his eye . . . something dark there. Dangerous."

Mrs. Pierce's words caught Alec by surprise. "I wouldn't really call it dangerous," he said, "but now that you mention it, I have been noticing something different about him lately." Alec shrugged. "Who knows what it is? Maybe something is in the wind. All the horses seemed on edge today."

"It's more than that," she said.

"He's been a good boy, for the most part," Alec told her. "I've seen a good bit of him this past week. There was one time, though, that I wasn't so sure."

Alec recalled to Mrs. Pierce the time Silver nearly knocked him over the cliff out by the far pasture. "Surely it was an accident and the pony was just playing around," Alec said finally. "It gave me a scare at the time, though. We should never have been out that close to the cliff in the first place."

Mrs. Pierce sighed. "He seems gentle enough with the girl, I suppose."

"He's her Prince Charming," Alec said.

The old woman shook her head. "It's not for me to say, but I'd be careful with him."

"Never a bad idea with any horse," Alec said. "I think Mora is smart enough to see that."

Back at the farm, Alec carried the victory blanket of flowers to the barn and set it on a bench by the door. Bartley came out of the barn office and listened in amazement as Alec described the wild start of the race and Silver's ultimate victory.

"I never would have believed it," Bartley said.

"I'm sure she'll tell you all about it when she gets here," Alec said. "She should be along any minute now."

19

THE TAKEN

"I WONDER WHAT'S keeping her," Alec said. It was ten minutes later and Mora and Silver still hadn't returned to the farm from town. After another ten minutes, he started to worry. Perhaps Silver had started acting up again, he thought. Perhaps she'd fallen, or been thrown. "I better try to find her," Alec said finally. "She should have been back by now."

Bartley stopped him just as he was about to mount up. "You don't think the kid decided to run off with the pony somewhere, do you?" Bartley asked. His voice was soft and sounded concerned.

"What do you mean?" Alec said. "Like run away from home?"

Bartley gave a slight nod. "Kids her age get some strange notions sometimes. You know how she feels about that pony," he said. "Maybe she did something foolish."

Alec shook his head. "She wouldn't do that. Not

Mora. Besides, what would be the point? With the money she won at the race, she should be able to buy Silver outright."

"Maybe," Bartley said. "But maybe not. After winning the race, the pony might attract a buyer that could outbid her. And who can say if her parents will really agree to her plan?"

"She seemed all right when we left her," Alec said. "I thought she was following right behind us. But after the way Silver was acting up at the start of the race, it does have me concerned a little bit."

"Not to worry," Bartley said. "She's probably just dawdling."

"If she turns up here before I find her, you better tell her to call Sharon."

"Of course," Bartley said. "Off with you now."

Soon Alec was turning the Black up the lane and onto the road to town. Arriving at the fair, Alec asked around for Mora but no one had seen her since right after the race. Again he wondered what could have happened to her. Perhaps she had simply taken the beach route home and he'd missed her coming from the other direction.

On the way back to the farm, Alec eased the Black off the road and down to the beach. This stretch of the beach was still covered with tracks scarring the sand after the race. He jogged the Black along the trampled sand until he discovered a place where one set of hoof-prints began tracking the opposite direction to all the rest. Alec was no expert trail scout, but the oval-shaped prints certainly looked like they could belong to Silver.

Before long the hoofprints broke off from the others and struck out on their own. Following the tracks, Alec reached the cutoff back to the farm. But instead of turning to the path through the dunes and back to the road to the farm, the tracks kept going. He trailed them all the way to the far point, where they vanished among the rocks.

As he watched the waves crashing on the rocks edging the point, the idea struck him suddenly that if Mora had ridden around the point for some reason, she could have become trapped on the other side when the tide started coming in. The cove around the point was completely inaccessible now, except perhaps by boat, and it would remain so until late that night when the tide went out again.

Alec decided that if Mora still hadn't shown up by the time he got back to the farm, he'd call the police station and tell them about his idea. Maybe the police could send a boat to see if Mora was trapped over there. Even if they couldn't land the boat in the heavy surf, they should still be able to determine if she was trapped there or not.

Alec let his gaze drift out to sea where the surface

of the ocean reflected the afternoon sunlight like the flashing of polished silver. A flock of seabirds was circling offshore and diving down upon a school of fish roiling a patch of water. His attention slowly returned to land again and Alec noticed the figure of someone emerging from between the dunes and walking down to the water. It was Mike Malloy, his long-tailed overcoat flapping around his legs in the wind. The old fisherman with the rusty gray beard stopped at the water's edge and stared out to sea. He didn't have his fishing rod with him today, but gnarled pieces of driftwood protruded from the bag slung over his shoulder.

Alec dismounted and led the Black over to him. "Well, stone the crow, if it isn't the Yank," Mike said.

"How are you doing, Mike?" Alec said.

"Well enough. How's yourself?" His face was smiling and open. The tips of his bushy eyebrows curved upward over his blue eyes like tiny, pointed horns.

Alec nodded to the sticks in the bag hanging from Mike's shoulder. "Are those for your carvings? Find anything promising?" he asked.

Mike shrugged his shoulders. "A couple pieces. Not much."

"By the way," Alec said, "you haven't seen a girl on a horse ride by here recently, have you? She's about twelve years old, riding a gray pony and wearing a blue sweater and brown riding cap?"

Mike tilted his head thoughtfully. "Is that the girl that won the horse race in town?"

"That's right," Alec said.

Mike nodded. "I think we've met. I used to see her out walking on the beach in the morning. Never saw her with a horse, though. Riding a gray pony, you say?"

"Silver gray. A mixed breed. Chunky. Not too tall. I don't know much about him, really. She found him wandering on the beach out by the point about a week ago. She's been keeping him at the Dailey farm."

Mike's eyes widened. "She found that horse on the beach? Here?"

"That's right," Alec said. "Hard to believe, I know. Anyhow, the girl never came home and I'm still looking for her. I found some tracks back there and was a little worried that she may have been trapped on the other side of the point by the tide," Alec said.

The old fisherman nodded back toward the point. "More likely she was taken," he said, "if she found the horse on this beach."

"Taken?" Alec asked. "What do you mean?"

"Just that, lad," Mike said. "Taken away."

"Like kidnapped?"

"No," Mike said. He turned to Alec, the expression on his face long and solemn. "Like taken away."

"Taken by whom?" Alec asked.

The man's bushy gray eyebrows arched over his eyes like ragged quotation marks. "By *him*, lad," Mike said. "By *him*. She's not the first."

Alec waited for the old man to explain. To Alec, Mike looked as if he was considering whether or not to say more, as if the right words were eluding him. He sighed and shook his head.

"Who are you talking about?" Alec said. "What are you talking about?"

"The child is lost," Mike said mysteriously. "You won't see her again, I imagine. She is with the kelpie now."

Alec laughed. "Is that supposed to be Silver? You're telling me that gutty little pony is one of these magical kelpies of yours? Before you said the Black looked like a kelpie. Don't tell me you can't see that Silver and a stallion like the Black are two very different animals! And before that you claimed a man in the tavern was a kelpie. And I heard another story about a kelpie in some lake and he was supposed to be white. So which is it?"

"Sure enough, the kelpie does look much like this black stallion of yours, in the creature's natural state.

That is, if one can say he has a natural state. Remember, the kelpie is a shape-shifter and able to change form at will."

Alec tried not to sound too surprised at what he was hearing. "So you were serious when you said you saw a kelpie in the tavern the other night?"

"Certainly. His kind still likes to pop into the pub for a pint from time to time."

Alec smiled and played along. "So how did you know he was a kelpie?"

"The seaweed in his hair, like I said before. Sometimes there are the marks of gill slits on his neck. Think what you want, lad," Mike said. "But if that horse was a kelpie, the girl is lost."

Alec looked into Mike's icy blue eyes, trying to judge if he was really joking around. From all Alec could tell, the man was deadly serious. What had he said about gill slits? Alec thought. All at once he recalled the crescent-shaped marks on Silver's neck. How could Mike know about them? He'd said he'd never even seen the pony before. Or had he?

Again Alec tried to read the eyes beneath the crooked eyebrows for some clue telling him this was only a joke, another story to peddle to gullible tourists, like Mrs. Pierce's "psychic readings." Mike stared back at him, his sober expression betraying nothing.

"I've seen some strange things in my life," Alec said, "but a horse that lives underwater and kidnaps people . . . I'm sorry."

Mike shook his head. "Think what you want. His kind won't die off just because people stop believing in him."

"Come on, Mike," Alec said. "I wasn't born yesterday. Besides that, I've heard these stories before."

Mike rubbed the rusty gray whiskers on his chin and sighed. "Sure, you're thinking old Mike is off his head. That's to be expected. But this isn't New York, lad. You're in Ireland. Always remember that. What's more, you are in the west of Ireland. The shape-shifters live among us here," he said. "I've seen them with my own eyes."

"Uh-huh," Alec said, playing along. "So if Mora was taken away by one of these shape-shifters, or kelpies, or whatever you call them, how do you get her back?"

"You don't. The girl is under the kelpie's sway now, probably trapped in one of his underwater caves beneath the reef. And there she will remain as long as the kelpie wants to keep her. The kelpies are as all-powerful as any being that ever walked the earth or swam the seas."

"All-powerful?" Alec said. "You're saying no one can get the best of him?"

"In the water nothing can defeat him," Mike said. "He draws strength from the sea. On land the kelpie's power resides in his saddle and bridle, particularly the bridle."

"His bridle?"

"That's right," said the old fisherman. "If a person can get a kelpie's bridle away from him, the power of his spell may be broken. But that is the only way. Aye, lad, many a brave soul has taken hold of a kelpie's bridle, but few have been able to get it away from him. Those that try are more likely to be dragged into the sea to their doom."

The Black pulled back, impatient to get going. "That's a great story, Mike," Alec said. "I'll keep it all in mind the next time I see the pony."

"Oh, you won't see him again," Mike said, eyeing the Black warily. "Not unless he wants to be seen. The kelpie finds you. You do not find him."

Alec stepped closer to the Black and gathered up the reins in his hands. "Oh, I'll find him, all right," Alec said. "But for now, you'll have to excuse me. I have to get going. The girl's probably waiting for me back at the farm as we speak."

Alec led the Black a few steps away, then pulled himself up into the saddle and set off back to the farm.

"Good day to you, then, and all the best," Mike called after him. "But watch your step, if you want my advice. Like I told you before, the only thing that devil covets more than a beautiful young girl is a beautiful black horse like himself. A stallion like your Black would tempt him mightily."

"Thanks for the warning," Alec said. He was going to say something else, and then thought better of it. He eased the Black ahead. "And just in case you're wrong, and you do see the girl on the beach somewhere, tell her to get home, would you please? Her folks will be getting worried."

Mike shook his head but didn't answer. Alec rode on. After a moment he turned to look back over his shoulder. The old fisherman was looking in the other direction, wading into the shallows to retrieve a piece of driftwood floating there, dragging the tails of his coat in the water.

On the way home Alec thought about what Mike had said. It troubled him more than he wanted to admit, especially in this place with its ancient myths, its fairy rings of standing stones, its fields where farmers wouldn't farm and coves where fishermen wouldn't fish.

There was still no sign of Silver or Mora when Alec arrived at the Dailey farm. He turned the Black loose in his pasture and then went down to the barn. Bartley was sitting at his desk in the barn office reading a magazine.

"Hear anything new?" Alec asked.

Bartley shook his head. "Not a word. The girl's aunt called here, though. She's a mite peeved, as you can imagine."

Alec told Bartley about his conversation on the beach with Mike Malloy. Bartley smiled wryly. "That rascal? A bit off in the head, he is. Never the same since his wife died."

Alec nodded. "Mrs. Pierce told me the same thing. Anyway, he seems friendly enough. But some of the things he was saying . . ."

Bartley chuckled. "Those old fishermen hereabouts will spin you a yarn, all right. They'll tell you they can see omens in the flights of birds, or read your future in the entrails of a fish. The country folks around here are a superstitious lot. I'm from Dublin originally. Things are a wee bit different there."

"Well, I'll tell you what I think," Alec said, picking up the phone. "I think Mora and Silver were caught by the tide on the other side of the point. We rode over there once before and I can see how it might happen."

Alec put in a call to the local police station. When he suggested sending a boat to check on the cove around the point, the officer thought it was a good idea. The officer said he'd put out an alert to their local patrols, but the law required they wait until morning before beginning an all-out search. Hopefully the girl would show up before then.

"Does the girl have many friends?" the policeman asked. "A boyfriend, perhaps?"

Alec understood the implication. "No, I don't think that's it," he said.

"I only ask because the last time we had a case like this, we found out later that the girl ran off to the city for a few days to see her fella."

"Not this time," Alec said. He thanked the man and hung up the phone.

After a few more minutes, Bartley said he had to be getting home. Alec told him he'd be in touch if there was news about Mora. Bartley left and Alec went into the house, where Mrs. Pierce was sitting at the kitchen table. She looked up from the magazine she was reading. "Has Mora not shown up yet?"

"Still gone," Alec said. "I think she may have gone for a ride on the beach and gotten stuck on the other side of the point when the tide came in."

"Hope she's all right," Mrs. Pierce said.

"The police are looking for her," Alec said. "I just spoke with them. They think she may have run off somewhere."

"I guess that's possible."

Alec pulled out a chair and sat down at the table. "I don't know what to think," he said. "I just saw

Mike Malloy down on the beach. He was telling me about those kelpies of his again. According to him, the pony is a kelpie and has carried off Mora to some underwater cave under the reef."

Mrs. Pierce took a sip of coffee from a cup at her elbow. "Would you like a cup?" she asked.

Alec shook his head. "No thanks."

"Mike is a great talker," Mrs. Pierce said, idly thumbing through her magazine.

"He did mention one thing that struck me as really unusual," Alec said.

"Just one, eh?"

"Mike was talking about some special power that resides in the kelpie's bridle. Maybe it's just a coincidence, but the pony really did seem to change when he was tacked up with that Mexican-looking saddle and bridle Olivaros left here. There was always something a bit off about the pony, but not like that."

"You say that bridle and saddle the pony was wearing weren't Tom's?" Mrs. Pierce asked.

A horse whinnied outside, but when Alec glanced out the window again he saw nothing new. "No," he said. "The tack belonged to Olivaros. He left them here when he came by before the race."

Mrs. Pierce shook her head. "Something odd about that, lad."

"I'd certainly like to talk to that man," Alec said.

"I think the police might want to have a chat with him as well."

"We'll see," Mrs. Pierce said. "I'll tell you one thing, though. If it turns out the girl simply took off somewhere, I wouldn't want to be in her shoes when her aunt Sharon gets hold of her. I spoke with her earlier and she's not happy about any of this."

"Don't suppose there is much we can do about it," Alec said.

"Don't suppose there is," Mrs. Pierce agreed. She picked up her magazine and returned to her reading.

Alec went upstairs to get cleaned up. When he came back downstairs again, Mrs. Pierce was gone. He ate his dinner, cleaned up his dishes, then walked outside to the Black's pasture. The clouds along the southwestern horizon had rolled closer, threatening to snuff out the last traces of painted afterglow in the sky over the southern sea. It looked like a storm was blowing in, Alec thought, and it was headed this way. He caught up with the Black and led the stallion back to the barn. Over toward town he heard the sound of fireworks and the strains of distant music.

There was a chill in the air, so Alec decided to walk back to the house and warm up with some hot tea. The horses were quiet enough now, despite the occasional crackle of fireworks coming from town. As he sat sipping his Earl Grey in the living room, a low booming sounded from outside. At first he thought it was more fireworks at the fair. But no, he realized quickly, it must be thunder ahead of the storm.

The phone rang and Alec picked it up. It was the police officer. "Any news on the girl?" Alec asked hopefully.

"I'm afraid not, lad," he said.

"How about around the point?" Alec asked. "Were you able to get a boat to take a look over there in case she was caught by the tide?"

"That's what I'm calling about," the officer said. "We just had word from harbor patrol a few minutes ago. They motored in as close as they could and looked the place over with binoculars. No sign of any-one there. No tracks even, or manure in the sand."

"I see," Alec said.

"Believe me," the officer said, "we are doing everything we can. If she's lost or up the coast some-where, we'll just have to hope she has the good sense to get in out of the storm. It looks like we have some weather coming in."

Alec thanked the man and hung up the phone. He walked across the room to gaze out the dark window toward town just as another wave of thunder rumbled in the distance. Soon a gentle rain began pattering on the slate roof.

Too bad, he thought. It looked like the last night

at the fair would be rained out. A flash of lightning bleached the sky. Out along the coast he could see the faint glow from smoldering bonfires on the beach.

Alec looked out toward the barn. All seemed quiet there, but after a moment he decided he'd better go out to the barn to check on the horses. He pulled on a raincoat from the hall closet and then dashed out into the rainy night, an umbrella in one hand and a flashlight in the other.

The air felt silky and thick and tasted of the sea. Ominous blue-black clouds hung low in the dark sky. Alec looked toward Oorloch and saw few lights at the fair and no sign of the bonfires that had lit the beach earlier.

Whipped by the wind, rain flew in a wild frenzy across the yard. More rain spilled from the gutters and danced in streams along the walkway until the stone drains took it away. Alec hurried the short distance between the barn and the house and then ducked into the barn and down the aisle to the Black's stall. Over the half door he could see the Black bobbing his head over the feed trough, whiffing at the remains of his dinner oats. Opening the latch, Alec stepped inside. The stallion moved to him and snuffled his nose into Alec's pockets, looking for treats.

"Easy, boy, easy now," Alec said, letting the Black

take a piece of carrot from his hand. He stayed with his horse awhile, talking to him gently and reassuring him the storm would be over soon. Suddenly there was a loud clap of thunder and Alec could hear whinnies of distress sounding from the other end of the barn. Leaving the Black, Alec started up the aisle to see if he could help quiet the others.

All the horses seemed a bit restless tonight, he thought, even the Black. It wasn't very surprising, really, not with the storm outside and the noise from the fireworks in town earlier. After settling Quackers and the others as best he could, Alec returned to the Black's stall. In the tack room he found a broom and started sweeping up the barn aisle, just to keep busy. The Black hung his head over the half door, watching him.

Soon the worst of the storm seemed to pass. The rain began to slacken and the rolls of thunder faded. Alec thought about going back to the house but, after a moment, changed his mind. He wasn't very tired, and the restlessness of the horses still bothered him. If he spent the night in the barn, at least he could keep an eye on them. And something told him that the barn might be the first place Mora would come if she did show up that night, at least if she was still with Silver.

Alec walked over to the tack room and found stable blankets and a fold-up cot. Outside he heard another wave of heavy wind and rain descend upon the farm suddenly. As he listened to the sounds of the storm, his thoughts turned to Mora again. Thinking he heard a noise at the other end of the barn, Alec looked up, half expecting to see Mora coming through the barn door. He waited but soon realized no one was there.

The Black, Quackers and the other two horses in the barn were all quiet now, backed deep into their stalls with their heads turned against the wall. Alec set up the cot in the aisle, just to one side of the Black's stall. Then he unfolded the blankets and made himself comfortable. This wouldn't be too bad, he decided. The blankets were thick and warm and a tack trunk sheltered him from the drafts blowing down the barn aisle. He found a newspaper he'd been reading earlier and thumbed through it to see if he could find something of interest there, settling on another story about the pair of whales that had beached themselves up the coast last month.

As Alec read, he could hear the Black rustling his feet in the straw bedding covering the floor. Puffs of cool air blew between the big sliding doors on either side of the barn. A lightbulb hanging from a wire in the rafters swayed in the draft, making the barn shadows move on the walls.

Alec tried to concentrate on the article he was reading, but his thoughts kept drifting back to his conversations with Mrs. Pierce and Mike Malloy that afternoon. Somehow ghost stories like that weren't so easy to dismiss at night as in the light of day.

Especially the part about the bridle, Alec thought. Was it really just a coincidence that all this trouble with Silver seemed to start when Olivaros showed up with his saddle and bridle?

So many strange things had happened since then that Alec didn't know where to begin counting them all. From the very first there was that stinging, electric charge that knocked him to the ground when he was saddling the pony. Then there were the physical changes to Silver, the weird growth spurt and swelling muscles, and the weird goo that seemed to grow on the saddle. Even the Black seemed to sense the change in Silver, and the other horses in the race had shied away from the pony from the very start.

Alec recalled what Mike had said about the telltale signs of gill slits and couldn't help but think of the scars on Silver's neck and the identical ones he'd seen on Olivaros. Could the horse and the man really be one and the same? Alec wondered. He had never seen the two of them together. As crazy as it sounded, it did sort of make sense.

Alec looked toward the Black's stall and took comfort in being near his horse. A voice in his head told him that whatever happened, the best thing he could do would be to stay close to the Black right now.

Soon the print on the page seemed to blur. A minute later his heavy eyelids were closing. He lay his head down on his cot, pulled up his blanket and began to doze. Dream images came into his mind like people crowding an empty room.

It felt like he'd been asleep only a few minutes, but when he woke and looked at his watch it was already four. All was quiet outside, he noticed. The rain had stopped and even the wind seemed calm now. The predawn air was cool on his face but Alec felt warm under his blankets, too comfortable to get up and go back to the house and make break-fast just yet. He rolled over and listened to the soft rasp of the Black's snoring in his stall, a slow qua-vering sound that began to lull Alec back into his dreams.

As he lay there, another sound began to mix with his horse's soft snoring. It sounded like a voice, per-haps a girl's voice, and familiar somehow, with words Alec couldn't make out. In his dreamy state of mind, whatever she was saying all seemed perfectly natural in some way. And then, somehow, it changed, becoming more like a cry for help.

What was that? Alec wondered suddenly, shaking himself awake. Who was that? With a jerk, he sat up and threw off his covers, his heart racing. "Mora?" he called. "Is that you?"

Alec looked around him, listened for the calling voice he thought he'd just heard beneath the buzz of the stallion's gentle snoring. But now there was nothing there. He listened a minute, then decided he simply must have been dreaming.

Pulling up the covers again, Alec took a deep breath and lay back on his cot. It was a little scary, waking up to find himself all alone in the dark barn, especially with so many ghost stories fresh in his memory. Maybe what he'd heard was some Irish ghost spirit channeling through the sleeping horse.

Don't be silly, he told himself. Next you'll be jumping at shadows and noises in the night. Hadn't he been in much more dangerous places before—the desert, the mountains, the Everglades, lost on a desert island, places with real threats to face? What was there to fear here?

Just as he was beginning to doze off again, a piercing cry from the Black jolted him awake. "Whoa, Black. Whoa!" Alec called instinctively. He jumped up and unlatched the door to the Black's stall. The stallion was backed into the far corner of his stall, tossing his head, his eyes wide and bulging.

"It's okay, boy," Alec said. "It's okay." The Black shrilled again and the cries and whinnies of the other horses answered him from the other side of the barn. In seconds the whole place was filled with the sounds of horses neighing and thrashing about in their stalls.

"Easy, boy," he said. "It's just me. Easy now. You're getting everyone all worked up." And then Alec heard it, that voice from his dream, mixed in with the shrill cries of the horses. It was a frightened, wailing cry for help, distressed, even desperate. Alec stopped talking to his horse and listened. He couldn't be just imagining things this time, not from the way the horses were acting. Then he heard something else, the sound of hoofbeats rushing by outside.

Alec jammed on his shoes, latched the stall door, ran toward the barn door and threw it open. He strained his ears to locate the source of the hoofbeats trailing off into the night. Outside the barn the air was wet and still. The storm clouds were gone now, the full moon shining brightly. He stared after the sound of the hooves until he made out something moving over the moonlit lane. It looked like the figure of horse and rider riding away down the lane and along the pasture fence.

"Stop. Hey, stop," he called. "Mora, is that you?"

Alec watched, and as if in answer to his call, the horse and rider pulled up, turned around and started back to the barn at a slow trot.

Quickly the ghostly shape began picking up speed, coming closer and closer. Alec could see it was Mora astride Silver, and they were bearing down on him. Along with the patter of hoofbeats Alec could hear the clatter and tinkling of the bells that hung on Silver's saddle strings, like wind chimes jingling in a breeze. The smell of seaweed tinged the air.

Mora must have lost her riding hat, as now her hair flew about her head and shoulders. She was hunched low over the pony's back. Her forearms were thrust deep in Silver's mane, a mane that seemed to hold her arms there like a nest of snakes. The lower half of her body was settled deep in her saddle, almost as if she was being swallowed into it.

Alec threw up his hands. "Whoa," he cried. "Slow down, Mora. Slow down." But Silver just kept coming, as if intent on running Alec down. Alec jumped out of the way as Mora and Silver jostled past. He watched in stunned disbelief as they rode off toward the beach. Again he heard the tinkle of the bridle bells mixed with the sound of hoofbeats splashing through rain puddles. Alec started after her a minute, but quickly realized it was no use. He stopped, turned around and ran back to the barn.

In seconds he was inside and yanking open the door to the Black's stall. He brought the Black outside. Taking hold of two fistfuls of mane, he pulled himself up onto the Black's back and pointed him up the driveway.

"Go, Black," he cried. "Go."

20

A NIGHTMARE
IN BLACK

SOON ALEC AND the Black were racing down the lane, chasing after the fleeting shadows in the night. Alec's eyes were adjusting to the dark now and he could just make out the girl and her horse as they crossed the road and set off past the moonlit dunes to the beach.

The wind whipped his face, heavy with the acrid smell of wet seaweed. Alec pressed himself low to the Black's neck as the stallion galloped along, guiding him with leg pressure and the touch of his hands. He could just make out the figures of Mora and Silver up ahead as they turned toward the far point.

Alec sat tight as they crossed the sleeping dunes and angled across the beach to the sea, the full moon hopping along beside them as the Black charged ahead. The stallion leveled out as they reached the hard-packed sand down by the water's edge.

Mora and Silver were only about one hundred yards away and the Black was closing on them fast. The white, moonlit beach was all the wider now with the dead low tide. The Black burst ahead, his hooves skipping over the sand, steadily drawing closer to the runaway girl and her horse. The stallion's thundering breath rang in Alec's ears. Cold salt air filled his lungs and chilled his skin.

Alec drew strength from his horse and urged the stallion on. The cliffs loomed closer as Mora and Silver reached the rocks on this side of the point. In an instant, horse and rider vanished into the moonlit shadows darkening the bottom of the high cliffs. Alec called out to Mora. His voice echoed back to him, bouncing down from the dark cliffs, first coming from in front, then in back, then from the direction of the sea.

Alec looked out to the point. With the full moon and extra-low tide, the passage through the rocks was plainly visible. He pulled up the Black and called again. Only more echoes answered him.

With no time to think, Alec urged the Black forward. The pony's tracks were easy to follow over the bright, moonlit beach. They led around the rocks and disappeared under the shadowy balconies of stone looming overhead to finally reemerge on the other side of the point. All was quiet save for the sounds of the

Black's deep breath and the crash of the surf. There was no sign of the pony or Mora.

Out to sea a glittering pathway of reflected light led out to the big full moon lowering on the western horizon. Closer to shore, towering columns of rock framed either side of the cove. The rotten egg smell of seaweed at low tide was even stronger on this side of the point, so strong it gagged in his throat like gas fumes.

Wincing at the smell, Alec followed the tracks as they crossed the sand to the water's edge and then vanished into the wash from the waves. He strained his eyes and ears, listening for some telltale sound, searching the wide, walled-in beach, sweeping his gaze from the water all the way up to the edge of the great cliffs. After a minute he saw what he took to be Mora and Silver standing on a patch of sand between two rock pillars that formed a twenty-foot-wide portal gating the sea. He rode closer but soon realized what he saw was only a shadow from the rocks.

Suddenly there was a sound behind him. It was a voice, not Mora's voice but a low, masculine laugh. Alec turned and, not ten yards away, saw the shape of someone stepping out of the shadows. The person seemed to come out of nowhere, startling even the Black.

The Black half reared and whirled around in a

circle. Alec slid down from the stallion's back and stepped in front of the Black, trying to keep some control over his horse. The stallion tossed his head, eyeing the stranger suspiciously.

Alec looked closer and recognized Olivaros, the supposed gypsy who claimed to be Silver's true owner. The man wore no coat, only a dark, heavy-looking sweater and dark, wet-looking pants that glistened in the moonlight like wet fish scales. Drops of water dripped from his silver-white beard. His long, stringy hair was pulled back from his neck.

Alec walked closer and could clearly see the pair of tattoolike markings on the gypsy's neck. In the yellow moonlight, the curved lines looked like slashes from a knife cut just below his ears, like fresh wounds that dripped no blood.

The Black shrilled loudly and pulled back. Without even a halter, the stallion was beyond Alec's control. All Alec could do to calm the Black's fury was spread his arms and put himself between them. Pressing his back against the Black's chest, Alec faced Olivaros.

"You? What are you doing here?" Alec demanded. "Where is the girl? Where is Mora?"

"Patience, lad," the man answered calmly. He would not look at Alec and kept his eyes on the Black. "She is with the others now." His voice was almost pleasant, like the heavy purring of a cat, yet sinister as well.

"With the others?" Alec said. "What others? Where is she?" He stepped forward angrily. Olivaros turned his gaze from the Black to Alec. He raised his arms above his head. The roar of the surf seemed to rise up with them. It startled Alec and he stopped in midstep. Olivaros raised his face to the sky, and then turned his cold, hard gaze upon Alec again.

"I sense your fear, boy," Olivaros purred. "Your heart is full of dread." The man turned his piercing gaze to the Black again and beckoned to the stallion. "Come to me, Black," he said. "Come. Join me. . . ."

The Black screamed. It was a shrill challenge that cut through the air like a blast of winter wind, a stark cry of cold, heartless fury. His forehooves stirred the sand at his feet, and then he lunged quickly, pushing Alec aside, his neck straight and outstretched like a sword, the whites of his eyes bulging.

Olivaros took a few steps back as the Black reared before him. Alec caught up to the Black and held the stallion still as best he could. Olivaros's face was calm, smiling. He spoke low words in a language Alec did not understand, an incantation directed to the Black. Whatever the words meant, the stallion wanted no part of them. The stallion lunged again, then stopped short, shaking his head and mane viciously.

The gypsy's face hardened. "Do not resist, my brother," he said, switching to American-accented English. It was a voice much like Alec's own. Alec could have sworn he was listening to himself as he heard the words coming out of the man's mouth, saying, "Easy, boy. Come with me, Black. Come."

The Black reared high in front of the mad gypsy, screaming his defiant scream, but he did not strike. Wind roared from his massive lungs as he beat the sand with his hooves. His body trembled with fury.

Olivaros looked startled for a moment, then the smile returned to his lips. He laughed and back-stepped away from the stallion, retreating down to the water's edge. "You dare to defy me?" he said, his voice deep and commanding again. "Here? In this place? Willing or not, you will come."

Another gush of sea air washed over them. The smell of the rotting seaweed in the air became so powerful that the stench of it caused Alec to double over, coughing and choking so that he could barely remain on his feet. When he looked again he saw Olivaros backing down to the water, then wading through the beach break and into the sea. His mad laughter echoed off the cliffs as the water rose over his waist. A moment later he leaned back to slip under the surface.

The dark water closed over him and he disappeared from view.

The Black held up at the water's edge, his body rigid with anger. The wind stopped suddenly. Alec stared offshore. He watched as a ripple appeared in a large, oily black swell rolling up toward the beach from the depths of the sea. As if cut by a shark's fin, the ripple became the point of the V-shaped wake slicing through the face of the swell. Phosphorus sparkles trailed behind it like a string of tiny lights. The swell rolled in closer, then stood up to become an exploding wave as it reached the shallows, a ball of white foam surging onto the beach. The wash from the wave rushed far up onto the sand, forcing Alec and the Black to scramble up the beach toward the cliffs.

A flash of lightning whitened the night, quickly followed by a booming clap of thunder. Alec saw something down by the shoreline in the trailing light. It was a horse and rider. It looked like Mora astride Silver. Or was it? Even in the bright moonlight he couldn't see the rider's face. Whoever it was, her hair was dripping wet and hanging in front of her face. Her bare upper arms were ghostly pale.

Silver, if it really was Silver, seemed different too. The color of his gray coat had changed, appearing so bleached out it was almost a luminous green color in the moonlight. His hindquarters were covered with a crustlike mantle of fish scales. Alec could hear a shelly rattling as Silver tossed his head and bucked.

Alec watched the girl shivering in the wet saddle. She was slouched forward, her hands lost in her horse's mane. Long strands of seaweed dangled like ribbons from her dark, wet hair. Her water-soaked clothes were plastered to her skin.

With a jerk, her head pulled to the side and the hair fell from her face. It was Mora, Alec realized now. Her eyes were glazed over, like a sleepwalker in a dream state. She sat motionless, transfixed, riveted to her saddle, her hands deep in the matted talons of dark mane.

"Mora," Alec called. Again the girl did not answer. Her breathing came louder, becoming a harsh rasp. She began to sway in her seat. Her mouth began to shake as if she was trying to speak but couldn't. Froth showed at the corners of her lips.

Silver started to move, slowly tracing a circle around Alec and the Black. Beside Alec, the Black pawed the ground, trembling with fury and fear. Alec stepped forward to reach out and take hold of Mora's arm. It felt almost limp in his hand, cold and wet. He gave a pull, but she stayed firmly seated in her saddle, as if glued to it. He pulled again, but Mora still did not try to help him, or give any indication that she even realized he was there.

"Mora," he called. "What are you doing?" Again no answer came from her shivering lips, only the guttural rasp of her breath. Then, finally, the rasp became a hoarse, pleading voice. The sounds spiraled out into the night, forming words Alec could finally understand.

"It's so cold," she was saying. "S-so c-cold. S-s-so c-cold."

Alec tugged desperately on Mora's arm, throwing his weight and trying to pull her out of the saddle. It felt as if he were trying to pull a limb from a tree. Mora's eyes rolled in her head. Suddenly she seemed to come alive, but only to resist him. Another flash of lightning illuminated her face. Her lips were pulled back now, her teeth bared. Her eyes, so glazed over before, were full of fire. With a shriek she threw Alec off. Silver wheeled around and broke away up the beach, taking Mora with him.

21

TO RACE THE KELPIE

ALEC VAULTED HIMSELF onto his horse's back and
the stallion lunged forward. Alec's mouth was dry, his
heart pounding. The heavy sound of galloping hooves
rumbled in his ears. Ahead of him he could see Mora
slouched over Silver, her forearms lost in the tangles of
wet mane. Her body jerked convulsively, as if racked
by brutal seizures.

The Black pulled alongside his rival. There was
only one way to stop them now, Alec knew. Reaching
out to take hold of the bridle, he could feel the horse's
hot breath on his hand. Above the cliffs there was a
sudden flash of lightning, followed closely by a boom
of thunder. As it faded, Alec could still hear Mora's
scream, but when he looked over his shoulder again,
she was no longer there. The runner and rider beside
him now seemed to be changing . . . becoming . . .
something else.

It seemed to Alec as if he were watching a film,

like a movie using high-speed, time-lapse photography. Beside him now he saw the flesh of both girl and horse fuse together. He could hear bones begin to crack. He saw muscles twist and wrench apart into pieces, re-arranging themselves, splicing together again.

Alec turned from the horrible vision and pressed his face close against the Black's neck, their racing hearts beating as one. Mora's bottomless scream deepened in his ears until it became a final, shattering roar. Alec gripped the bridle tighter in his hand. Whatever he thought he was seeing, it couldn't be real. Hang on, he told himself. Just hang on.

Something banged up against the side of his leg, something that felt like rough leathery hide. A heavy, bellowing sound filled his ears. Alec glanced up to see that Silver was no longer there, and neither was Mora. As impossible as it seemed, running beside him now was what looked like an enormous bull, a black bull, blacker than the night around it.

Moonlight shone on the bluish tips of the bull's horns and bared teeth. A great hump of bunched muscle rolled on the creature's back. A purple tongue lolled from a slobbering mouth that was pulled back into a horrible snarl. Dark seaweed hung from its chin and neck like a beard. Alec blinked. He closed his eyes and opened them again. The nightmare vision would not go away.

With fierce, prehistoric power, the bull twisted the great bulk of his body, pulling Alec and the Black closer to the water. Alec turned his face to the Black. Putting his cheek to the stallion's warm neck, he closed his eyes once more. His shoulder and arm strained against the force beside him, the bridle still clenched in his fist.

This must be some kind of waking dream, he thought. It just can't be real. No matter what his senses told him, no matter what he saw, smelled or felt, somehow he knew it just couldn't be real. When he opened his eyes again it would all be over.

Flying sand and sea spray stung Alec's face. He blinked his eyes open to see the bull swing his head viciously and lunge toward the Black. The stallion twisted out of the way just as the tips of the bull's gleaming horns slashed inches from the Black's head.

Alec threw himself forward on the Black's neck. As he did, he saw the bull's thick muscled forelegs begin to change shape, stretching now, becoming more slender, longer, and changing again. Alec turned his head away. His hand burned with pain. The bridle felt hot, as if it was about to burst into flames. Yet somehow he could not let go of it.

Again Alec's leg bumped against the hideous thing running beside them. But this time he did not feel the leathery hide of a bull brush against his ankle. It felt more like coarse hair. Alec blinked his eyes and his vision cleared. A rack of spiked antlers was shaking close to his face. Careening along next to him now was a black stag. The antlers crowning its head cut the air like great fingers of black coral.

The unearthly stag lashed out with its crown, tearing Alec's shirt and raking his arm. Alec could hear his shirt tearing and feel the pain. He blinked again. It was no use, he thought. He couldn't close his eyes and make any of this go away. All Alec knew for certain was that he was still riding the Black. That alone gave him the strength to hang on.

As the stag tried to drag him out of the saddle and into the water, it began to change shape once more, like a balloon with air squeezing about inside it. The head became larger and more angular. A thick forelock sprouted between the crown of horns, and a mane grew on its neck. The rack of antlers began retracting like telescopes folding in upon themselves, becoming smaller and smaller. They collapsed into two curved black horns, finally settling into the pricked ears on the head of a black horse. It was a black stallion, the mirror image of the Black himself!

Desperate thoughts flashed through Alec's mind. All at once, the words of the old fisherman came back to haunt him. Hadn't Mike Malloy said the murderous kelpie sometimes coveted horses as well as girls? Could it be that it was the Black the kelpie was really after, had been after ever since that first morning on the beach back in New York, and Mora was only the bait in the trap? Certainly this was the very horse he'd seen on the beach that morning on Long Island last month. Was it coincidence or fate that brought him to this place and time to run this final race against the kelpie, a race for life and death?

Alec could feel the Black trembling with fury now and the stallion's determination and anger gave him new strength. He would not allow himself or the Black to be dragged out into the sea by this thing, whatever it was, not while there was strength left in his body.

The Black put a head in front of his rival and Alec knew the time was now or never. Redoubling his grip on the burning bridle, Alec locked his fingers against what felt like the stinging of a swarm of angry hornets. Closing his eyes, he steeled himself against the pain. He heaved with all his weight, determined not to let go as the Black tried to edge the demon horse away from the water.

The kelpie came on again, and once more the two horses careened ahead as if tangled together in a single flying harness, the kelpie trying to drag the Black into the sea, the Black pushing back, fighting up the beach toward the safety of the land. Alec hung on, caught between them.

With one hand locked around the Black's neck

and the other clenching the bridle, Alec felt as if his body was about to be ripped apart. Directly in front of him, less than fifty yards away, were two high, columnlike rock pillars rising up from the sand, like an enormous stone gate. There was plenty of room to pass between the gate's pillars—if the horses would turn. But, as if in a battle of wills that would be played to the death, each horse held his ground, intent on driving the other into the rock.

The seaward pillar loomed up ahead. Alec gritted his teeth and desperately tried to pull up the horses from their mad, suicidal course. It was hopeless and Alec's mind raced, crowded with the unknowable thoughts people think when they believe they are within moments of a violent death. His breath was frozen in his lungs, his teeth clenched. The unstoppable horses rushed ahead, straight for the stone column at a full gallop.

If it had all been just a dream, this would have been the moment to wake up. Alec squeezed his eyes closed and then opened them again, trying to will himself awake, anything to get away from here. But all his senses told him this was not a dream. And he did not wake up.

"Now, Black. Now," he called to his horse, knowing he had but one hope to save himself. The Black answered Alec's cry with a final rush of speed, and for a split second the Black was again able to get a head in front. Alec yanked desperately at the burning bridle in his hands. With only inches to spare, the twin horses scraped between the barnacle-encrusted pillars, driving by it and up the beach toward the cliffs.

The demon horse screamed as they veered away from the water's edge. Alec threw himself forward, heaving upon the bridle with both hands and all his weight. Finally he felt something break between his fingers. He lost his balance and fell. The breath left his body as his back hit the ground. Then all went black.

22

the Light of Day

TIME PASSED, AND as his senses returned, Alec felt a soft pressure against his shoulder and smelled the familiar closeness of his horse. The Black was gently nudging him awake. Alec could hear the sound of the beach break close by, mixed with the Black's soft nickering. He raised his head from the sand and tried to focus his eyes.

The stallion was standing protectively beside him. The smell of seaweed lingered in Alec's nose and throat, along with the gritty taste of salt and sand in his mouth. He felt very thirsty.

The Black watched as Alec climbed unsteadily to his feet. Early-morning sunlight streaked over the beach. What was he doing here? Alec wondered.

He took a small step, then another. He tried to wipe the sand from his face and found his hands clenched into fists, as if his fingers were glued together. He worked to pry them open, and what looked like a piece of seaweed and a few shells fell out and dropped to the sand. Alec took no notice and continued trying to rub some life back into his cramped hands. His right hand felt like he'd been sleeping on top of it and all the blood was squeezed out. He kept rubbing and finally his fingers began to tingle and loosen up a little.

After a minute the Black started down toward the water and Alec followed after him. To one side was a single set of hoofprints in the sand that led across the beach to the water's edge. Aside from the horse's tracks, there were no signs that anyone save he and the Black had ever been here, certainly no sign of a bull or stag or anything like that. Overhead he could hear the cries of the seabirds as they darted and dove from their perches along the cliff face above. The morning sun cast long shadows from the cliffs down onto the beach.

Alec stepped into the water to splash water on his face and hands. Deep creases marked his right palm. He rolled up his shirtsleeves and noticed a long rip in the right sleeve. There was also a red scrape mark running up his right forearm. The scrape stung when he washed the raw skin with the salty water, and a shiver of pain shot up his arm. For some reason, Alec did not mind it. The pain was almost refreshing. Somehow it made him feel lucky just to be alive to feel it.

His legs wobbled beneath him as he splashed more water onto his face and over the back of his neck. Soon the cool water was making him thirstier than ever. Walking through the shallows, he staggered up onto the beach.

Alec sat down in the dry sand, took a deep breath and tried to collect himself. He still wasn't sure what had happened to him the night before, what was real and what wasn't. Half-formed dream images flashed through his mind, horrors that made him question his very sanity. There were unearthly visions of animals changing shape before his eyes, of slashing horns and pounding hooves. Certainly it was more than just some incredible nightmare, he told himself. Yet his waking mind also told him that what he remembered simply couldn't have been real.

But if it was all just a dream, how did he get out here to this lonely cove on the other side of the point? Could he really have been involved in some wild chase after Mora and Silver? Again he looked up and down the beach. Except for the single set of tracks leading into the sea, there was no sign that anyone besides him and the Black had ever been here.

Finding his feet again, Alec stood up. The Black came closer and stood beside him. Alec slid his hand over the Black's shoulder and spoke softly to his horse.

Whatever had occurred, Alec decided, he could only feel thankful to be alive to see another day, thankful that he and the Black were safe and that they would be leaving this place soon and heading home to the States.

After a moment the stallion moved away, turning his attention to a school of baitfish darting in the shallows. Out to sea a fishing boat was chugging its way back to the harbor at Oorloch. A whirling flock of gulls danced in its wake.

Alec rubbed his palms together. The burning numbness was easing now. He cupped his hands and blew on them to try to bring some more warmth into his fingers again. His gaze swept up the beach to where the single set of tracks not belonging to the Black led to the sea. He walked closer and bent down to get a better look. They were the oval-shaped tracks of a horse, an unshod horse with an overreaching stride, running straight into the water.

Alec backtracked all the way up the beach to where he'd found himself on the beach this morning. His bleary eyes caught the glint of something in the sand at his feet. He crouched down and realized it was the same object that had fallen out of his hand earlier, not shells and a strand of seaweed but a piece of leather fringe, about two inches long, strung with tiny pearls and shell-shaped silver bells.

Alec examined the string of tiny bells in his hand and watched as the beads caught the shining morning light like sparkling jewels. Certainly it was a bridle string, a piece of fringe torn from Silver's bridle, Alec thought. More important, it was proof that his memory of what had occurred last night wasn't all just some mad dream. The bells tinkled lightly as he rolled the string between his fingers. It was a haunting sound, even in daylight.

But if the race had been real, he asked himself, what had happened at the end? That part was still fuzzy in his mind. And Mora? Where was she now? Was she still with Silver or Olivaros or the kelpie or whatever it was? Had she ever even been there at all?

Alec looked around him. The beach was empty, yet even now he felt eyes upon him, as if they were not alone, as if they were being watched by some non-human presence. Shadows moved here and there. Was that a black seal swimming just offshore? he wondered. A black cat among the dunes? A black bird perched on the cliff? Were they even real animals? Or was it the kelpie following him, changing shape as he went along?

Alec looked at the piece of broken bridle string in his hand and then slipped it into his pants pocket. He blinked his tired eyes and took another deep breath, trying to clear his head again. This was crazy, he thought. All he wanted was to get away from this place, the sooner the better.

Turning his gaze to the north, and the way back to the farm, he could see that the tide was coming in already. All at once Alec realized he'd have to hurry if he didn't want to be caught on this side of the point. The Black seemed to sense the same thing and had already started walking along the water's edge in that direction.

Alec caught up with the stallion and together they made their way to the point and the path to the other side. They splashed through the ankle-deep water already washing over the path between the rocks. The Black took the lead, dodging between the waves and the rocks. In places, the waves came up higher, sometimes rushing all the way up to the base of the cliff.

Soon they were safe on the other side and walking along the shoreline, headed for the farm. The beach was as empty on this side of the point as it had been in the cove, not a person in sight anywhere. The wind blew from behind them now, as if hurrying them along.

When they reached the farm, Alec turned the Black loose in his pasture and hosed some fresh water into the trough. The stallion drank greedily and soon Alec joined him, cupping a few handfuls of water from the hose into his own mouth. It was wonderful to clear the taste of salt and seaweed from his lips.

After they finished drinking, Alec walked the Black down to the barn. He put the Black in his stall and scooped a serving of oats into his feed trough.

"Alec?" called Bartley from the other end of the barn.

Alec stepped out of the stall.

"I was wondering where you were off to, lad," Bartley said. "I saw the cot and blankets left out and . . . Hey, are you all right?"

Alec held up his hands. "I'm okay," he said. "I'm okay."

"What happened to you last night?" Bartley asked, looking Alec up and down.

Alec shrugged his shoulders. "To tell the truth, I'm not really sure. Whatever happened, I ended up on the beach this morning. Guess I took a spill somewhere along the line. I'm all right now. Just a little scraped up."

Bartley chuckled and shook his head. "A big night at the fair, was it?"

"No, nothing like that," Alec said. "I was sleeping in the barn and the horses woke me up. There was some noise outside and when I went to check on it I saw a horse and rider go by. Only they didn't stop, just kept right on going. I thought it was Mora and Silver, so I tried to catch up to them on the Black. We chased them down to the beach and . . ." Alec paused to consider telling Bartley more about last night, then thought better of it. He still wasn't sure what had happened himself. "Anyway," he said finally, "whoever they were, I lost them."

"Crazy kid," Bartley said. "And if you ask me, you're twice as crazy for chasing after her. Lucky you didn't fall off a cliff in the dark. You should be careful riding at night by yourself around here, lad."

"Believe me," Alec said, "I don't plan on doing it again."

Bartley just laughed and smiled at Alec. "Why don't you go inside and get yourself something to eat?" he said. "Take a shower. You look like you could use it."

Alec glanced down at his wet and sandy clothes and managed a laugh. "I guess you're right," he said, and walked across the driveway to the house.

The hot shower felt terrific, though the scrape on his arm stung when he washed it. Again his thoughts returned to last night. Whatever had happened, he thought, in the end, the girl was gone. And despite his overwhelming desire to simply get away from here and forget about it all, he couldn't stop feeling that somehow he was responsible for what had happened to Mora. It made him mad at himself. A voice in the back of his mind nagged at him, telling him Mora was still out there somewhere and he could do more to find her, that he knew better than anyone that the girl had not just run off to the city or spent the night camping out.

At least he could speak with Mora's dad and try to explain what happened, Alec thought. Then he had to laugh at himself. Explain what happened? And say what? That Mora had been kidnapped by a shape-shifting kelpie? That she was now lost, among the taken? Who could ever believe such a story? It sounded ridiculous.

After he got into some dry clothes, Alec scrambled a few eggs for breakfast. He threw his ripped-up shirt into the garbage. The pants he'd been wearing, still wet from last night, he hung out to dry on the clothesline. He turned the side pocket inside out and found the piece of tassel torn from the kelpie's bridle.

Alec turned the string over in his fingers. A sticky piece of seaweed clung to the wet leather fringe. It didn't look like much now, just a soggy piece of leather with a few silly ornaments attached to it. But hadn't Mike Malloy said that the bridle was the key to the kelpie's power? And here it was in his hand, or a piece of it at least. If what Mike said was true, maybe it could lead him to the kelpie again, and to Mora. Alec slipped the piece of tassel into his pocket. Maybe Mike could help, Alec thought, if he could find him in time. He started for the barn to get the Black.

There was no sign of Mike or anyone else on the beach. As he rode closer to Oorloch, Alec noticed a group of people gathered in a circle close to where a small fishing boat had just pulled in to the dock. Perhaps someone had landed a big fish, Alec thought. But then he saw there were flashing lights too. It was an ambulance.

Alec found a place to tie up the Black and ran up the steps to see what was going on. Making his way through the crowd, Alec saw that the group was gathered around someone seated on a dockside bench. Alec couldn't see much, with the men clustered around, just someone wrapped in a crumpled blanket. He pushed his way closer.

It was Mora. Her face was gaunt, her hair stringy and wet beneath the blanket draped over her head and shoulders. She was staring at the ground. Her eyes were glazed over and her shivering hands were clasped around a cup of hot tea steaming in a plastic cup. A medic from the ambulance stood beside her, talking on his walkie-talkie radio. Alec edged up to them. A man held him back. "Let her breathe, people," the man said. "Stay back. Give her some air."

"Poor thing must have been washed out to sea," someone said.

"Pure luck anyone found her," said someone else. "I hear she was hanging on to a marker buoy a mile offshore. Lord knows how she got there."

Alec ducked under the man's arm and called to Mora. She lifted her head and turned to the sound of Alec's voice. "Alec?" she rasped.

Alec pressed closer. "Are you okay?"

"Alec?" she rasped again, her eyes suddenly coming into focus and flashing with recognition. He took the cup from her shaking hands and held it to her lips.

"Take it easy, pal. Drink some of this," he said. She took a sip and then turned her face away.

"You okay?" Alec asked. "What happened?"

"I don't know," she said, finding her voice at last.

"You remember winning the race, don't you? And the prize money?"

Mora smiled. "Yes. I remember that. And I remember riding home from the race, and the fog that came out of nowhere. It was really thick. Didn't you see it? And then we got lost somehow. Everything was dark and wet and cold. I can't remember a thing after that . . . just the sound of waves and . . ." Mora's voice trailed off.

Alec put his hand into the pocket of his jeans and pulled out the piece of tassel torn from Silver's bridle. "Do you remember this?" he asked, holding it up to her face.

Suddenly Mora's eyelids began fluttering. Her shoulders slumped and she went limp. The medic touched Alec on the arm. "That's enough, son. We need to get her to the hospital before she goes into shock."

After the ambulance left, Alec untied the Black and started home along the beach. Soon he saw a familiar figure poking around in the shells by the water's edge. It was Mike. Alec told the old fisherman everything that had happened last night, or at least what he thought had happened. He showed him the bridle string. Mike listened to Alec's story and then shook his head. "You don't think the girl could have escaped the kelpie, do you? Surely you know that he let her go intentionally." Mike held up the bridle string and let it dangle between his fingers, rattling the tiny bells. "And the only reason he did so was because you have this." Mike handed the string back to Alec. "With this you will always have some hold over the kelpie," Mike said. "But be careful. He may have some hold over you as well."

Alec looked at the tasseled piece of fringe in his hand, wondering about the power it held, the power to summon the kelpie. Was there any way to control something like that? he asked himself. Even if there was, did he really want to be responsible for that kind of power?

"No thanks," Alec said, pushing the thing back to Mike. "I never want to experience another night like the one I had last night. You take it."

Mike shook his head and laughed. "Not me, lad. I'm old and happy with my life just the way it is. You're young, so I imagine you see things a mite different. But whether you know it or not, you made a bargain with the kelpie last night. If the girl was returned and is safe, it seems to me that the kelpie kept up his part of the deal. Now I'd say you'd be wise to keep yours."

Alec held out the bridle fringe. "You mean give this thing back to him?" he said. "No problem. He can have it. Right now I just want to get out of here and find someplace where I don't have to worry that every other animal I see isn't really some shape-shifting creature looking for a human being to torment."

Mike looked up at the Black, who was staring uneasily out toward the point. "That's probably not a bad idea right about now, though I wouldn't think you have to be too concerned on that score, not with a friend like this one here to look after you."

They talked another minute. Alec turned to go, but Mike called for him to hold up. "Wait a second, lad," he said. "I forgot to give you this, a wee souvenir of Ireland."

Mike reached into his shoulder bag and pulled out

a small object wrapped in newspaper. Alec unfolded the wrapping. It was one of Mike's driftwood chess pieces, a finely carved horse's head, the black knight, smooth and black as ebony.

When they reached the turnoff to the farm, Alec stopped, slid off the Black's back and walked down to the water's edge. He reached into his pocket and pulled out the bridle string, dangling it between his fingers. The little bells chimed softly in the breeze.

All at once the Black began dancing in place. The stallion tossed his head and glared up into the sky. Alec followed the stallion's gaze to a spot where a black bird was circling low overhead. Slowly the bird descended closer.

"I'm not afraid of you," Alec called out to the bird. The Black shrilled wildly. Alec steadied his horse, then held out the bridle string and called to the bird again. "I won this fair and square, but I give it back. All I want in return is for you to leave us in peace."

With that Alec threw the bridle string down in the wet sand at the water's edge. A wave swept over it and the backwash began pulling it out to sea.

The black bird hovered overhead and cawed. The Black tossed his head and shrilled a reply. The stallion broke away from Alec, rearing to paw the air as the bird dove down to snatch up the string in his beak.

Alec stepped closer to his horse. "Easy, boy," he said. "He's leaving. Let him go now." After a moment the Black settled again. They stood there together, Alec's hand on his horse's neck, watching as the black bird flew out across the bay, out to the heart of the sea.